Cass
and the
Stone Butch

Cass and the Stone Butch

Antoinette Azolakov

BANNED BOOKS
Austin, Texas

A Banned Book

FIRST EDITION

Copyright © 1987
By Antoinette Azolakov

Published in the United States of America
By Edward-William Publishing Company
P.O. Box 33280-#231, Austin, Texas 78764

ALL RIGHTS RESERVED.
No part of this book may be reproduced in any form without written permission from the publisher, except for brief passages included in a review appearing in a newspaper or magazine.

ISBN 0-934411-06-9

Library of Congress Cataloging-in-Publication Data

Azolakov, Antoinette, 1944–
    Cass and the Stone Butch.

    I. Title.
PS3551.Z66C37 1987 813'.54 87-24103
ISBN 0-934411-06-9

To
Anne Peticolas
and to
Lisa Carrie Brown,
with gratitude.

Chapter 1

"Where's Sharla?" Lisa had to lean over the table and shout for me to hear her, there was so much noise in the bar.

I shrugged my shoulders. I didn't care where Sharla was. She wasn't a friend of mine, I hardly knew her lover Lester at all, and at the time I never dreamed that Sharla's activities or Lester's investigations of them could ever be any concern of mine. I'd seen Sharla arguing with Lester on the dance floor earlier, but I hadn't paid much attention. They'd been arguing all the way to Houston, so it was nothing new. At least now that we were here, they weren't inflicting their differences on us at such close range. I'd nearly been ready to get out of Lisa's car and walk, for a while there.

Kelley and Elkhorn finished an exuberant dance and collapsed at the table, panting and grinning.

"Wow!" Elkhorn draped her arm over Kelley's shoulder, and they turned their faces toward each other and leaned their foreheads together, looking into each other's eyes. Their two heads of blonde hair were so nearly the same color that they looked like part of the same person where their short bangs touched, except that Kelley's hair was wavy and Elkhorn's was perfectly straight.

Lisa tapped Elkhorn on the arm and she turned, picking up her beer and saying, "Huh, what?" as she stopped with the bottle halfway to her lips.

"Have you seen Sharla?"

"No, why? Isn't she with Lester somewhere?"

"Lester's gone to the restroom to look for her. She thinks she's slipped out of the bar, though."

Kelley pulled the bottle away from Elkhorn and drank a slug herself. "Better get us another one, Kiddo," she said.

"Okeydoke." Elkhorn swung onto her feet and away through the crowd with a supple grace that still surprised me when I watched her. You'd never think somebody so long and lanky could move like that. She was really something to watch on the basketball court.

Lisa had turned in her seat and was scanning the dancers and the crowd around the bar along the back wall. This Houston bar was a lot different from the Hairpin Turn, our women's bar at home, and one of the big differences was that it was light enough to see across the room without getting terminal eyestrain. The lights were actually white instead of red. The decor of this place was white, too, or white and silver with black accents, very high-tech and Buck Rogers-looking, but okay for a change. And change was, after all, the main reason we'd all come down here from Austin for the weekend, anyway. I'd hoped that if Sharla Doyle, who was not my favorite dyke in the world any more than I was hers, was coming with us and bringing her teenage drag-butch lover, that they'd at least behave themselves out of consideration for the rest of us. That would have been a real change. They'd met about a month or two ago and to anybody's knowledge had done nothing but carry on big, dramatic fights ever since. No doubt they did manage to find common ground when they went home at night, but you couldn't tell it from their public behavior.

Lisa half-stood and peered through a temporary gap in the crowd of dancers. "Here comes Lester, anyway," she said, and I did indeed see Lester's stiff and self-conscious form moving toward us through the gyrating couples, arms at her sides and shoulders in her boy's sport coat rigidly squared. She arrived at the table and glared down at us without sitting down.

"You didn't see her?" Lisa asked, concern in her voice.

"No."

"Sit down, Lester." I patted the seat of the chair next to mine.

"Where the shit could she have gone, goddammit?"

"Who? Sharla?" It was Jacko, my best dyke friend in the world, who had come up behind me with her lover Tina on her arm. "She told us she was going to another bar."

"Oh, shit!" Lester clenched her fists and shook them. "Great! Just great!"

Jacko said, "Didn't she tell you?" and Lisa said, "Take it easy, Lester," while I said, "Jacko, did she say what bar?"

"I think she said the Orchid Room."

"Shit!" said Lester, still clenching her fists and now her jaw as well.

"Why, Lester? Do you know anything about it?" Lisa was trying to get some perfectly innocent and necessary information, but Lester turned a murderous look on her that made her recoil.

"Shit, yes, I know something about it. It's a goddamn men's bar, that's what! She's been wanting to go there ever since that faggot brother of hers told her about it. It's just a goddamn meat rack, that's what it is." She glowered at Jacko. "Who'd she go with?"

"Nobody, I guess. What she said was, 'I'm going over to the Orchid Room. I'll see y'all later.' "

"Oh, *shit!*"

I took hold of Lester's arm with one of my firmer grips. "Lester," I told her, "I'm going over there and find her and bring her back here, okay? So settle down and drink a beer or something and I'll be back."

I thought, in my innocence, that I might serve as the voice of sweet reason in the Lester–Sharla feud. I'd just go find Sharla, get her to come back and be civil, and we wouldn't be burdened with all this high drama any more. All I wanted was peace and happiness and good times for all. It made sense to me at the time.

I got up from the table and kissed Lisa on the cheek. "I'll be back in a little while, babe."

Lester, who had finally sat down and was covering her face with her hands in the classic pose of despair, jumped to her feet. "I'm going with you," she announced.

I shrugged my shoulders. "Fine. Come on." I started for the door and Lester came pushing along behind me, crowding my heels and nearly stepping on them in her angry haste.

When we got to the front door of the bar, I realized I wasn't a bit familiar with the Orchid Room and didn't have the slightest idea where it was. I turned to Lester, putting out my hand to stop her in her headlong rush. "Do you know where this place is we're going?" I asked her.

"Westheimer someplace, is all I know. How the hell were you going to find it if you didn't even know where it was?"

I turned to the woman checking ID's at the door and said, "Pardon me, but can you tell me where the Orchid Room is?"

"What?" Even in the vestibule by the door, the noise and the music were pretty loud. "Right back the way you came; you'll see the door with the sign on it."

"Huh?" The woman was pointing over the crowd toward the back of the bar. Light dawned. "No, not the restroom. The Orchid Room. It's a men's bar."

"The Orchid Room?"

"Yeah. Do you know how we can get there from here?"

"Oh, the Orchid Room. Yeah. Just go right over this way until you get to Westheimer, take a left, and it's about a block over that way. You can't miss it. It's a men's bar, though."

I gave her a smile. "Yeah, I know. Thanks a lot." Lester was already pushing her way out the door and onto the sidewalk. I followed her and caught up with her in a couple of steps.

"Well, it shouldn't be far, anyway," I said. "You aren't afraid to walk, are you?" To tell the truth, the big, strange city at night intimidated me just a little.

"Sharla walked." Lester set her jaw and strode out, making me almost trot to catch up with her.

The October night was clear and a little chilly, feeling good to me after the stuffiness of the over-warm bar. I hadn't worn a jacket and now I was glad. Lisa and I had argued about it when we were leaving Austin. She thought I'd freeze without one and I was just as sure I'd burn up in one and have to take it off and lug it around with me all night and probably lose it somewhere. I'd been right, and it was a good thing. I'd have rather died than admit I was cold, after all that.

We strode along the sidewalk together with Lester, who is a good deal shorter than me, taking about a stride and a half to my one. You could almost hear the anger every time her foot hit the ground.

"Nice night for a walk," I said.

"I wouldn't know."

"My favorite time of the year, October."

"Uh."

"I think I like it even better than March. So clean, or something. Such a relief after the summer."

"Uh."

"Of course, March is hard to beat after a cold winter. Soft and springy, and all that pale, goldy green. Everything growing, and that fresh-turned earth smell. And my birthday's then, too. When's your birthday?"

"January."

"Hm. Do you like January particularly well? I've wondered if everybody likes their birth month, or if I'm just lucky in mine."

"It's okay."

I looked at the grim-faced young woman at my side and studied her profile as we walked. The determined line of the jaw contrasted with the softness of the smooth cheeks, the strong line of the neck led up in the back to severely short but fine-textured hair as fluffy and white as cotton, and the tense body in the tailored men's clothes gave the same impression of muscular power a draft horse does. Not a heavy draft horse, but one a lot solider than a regular riding horse. I even knew a horse named Lester once, but he wasn't as nicely put together as this Lester was. This one looked just about like I wished I looked. I look fatter than that.

"Lester, what's the deal with you and Sharla, anyway?"

She glanced at me sharply and snapped her head back to the straight-ahead position.

"What do you mean?"

"Well, I mean, you-all haven't been getting along the best, have you? Is she seeing somebody else or something?"

"What's it to you?"

"Nothing. I just hate to see you beating your brains out over somebody when you could be having fun, that's all."

"Thank you, Mama Milam."

I sighed. "Okay, Lester, I know it's not my business—"

"Right. Good thinking."

"—but if she's not treating you right, there's a hundred women in any town that will."

"Yeah. Sure."

"Sure, for a fact."

We walked on. She didn't answer. We got to Westheimer, looked up and down the street, and spotted a purple glow coming from a building on our side of the street in the first part of the next block.

"Think that's it down there?" I asked.

"It better be," said Lester.

We set off down the block, passing two or three little groups of gay men, several of whom sported leather outfits, skin-tight and studded with nickel-plated hardware. Lester was ominously silent. I didn't know whether or not to hope we found Sharla in the Orchid Room so I could dump her surly lover with her and get away before the fight broke out.

We got to the Orchid Room and were challenged at the door by a man in leather jeans that looked like they'd been painted on with high-gloss enamel. A tiny vest of the same material was chained tightly together across his hairy chest, exposing more muscles than I'd ever seen in person before, along with some kind of tattoo on the right biceps which looked fascinating, but I didn't want to stare at it long enough to really make it out.

The guy looked Lester up and down.

"Can I see your ID, lady?" His voice was so deep it could have substituted for a sousaphone in the Longhorn Marching Band.

Lester glared at him. "Why? You gonna show me yours?"

I grabbed her arm, hard, and smiled ingratiatingly up at the leather hulk. "She's just a little touchy tonight," I told him.

"Yeah, well I got to see an ID or she ain't coming in here."

"Show him your ID, Lester."

"You show him yours! How come you don't have to show your goddamn ID all the time?"

The hulk flicked his glance over me and laughed. It was my turn to glare at him. He wasn't impressed.

"Just show him your goddamn driver's license and let's go in, will you? Sharla's probably out the back door by now."

This argument, far-fetched as it was, won the day, and Lester sullenly dug out her fake ID from the breast pocket of her sport coat and handed it over. The leather man scrutinized it under a lamp on the little desk beside him and handed it back.

"Six dollars," he said.

"Six dollars?" Lester shouted.

"Lester, shut up!" My voice overrode hers. To the doorkeeper I said, "You mean three dollars apiece?"

"Six." A man in a tee shirt and 501 Blues pushed past us and handed Leather Man three dollar bills. Leather Man grinned. I took six dollars out of my billfold and handed them to him along with a sweet smile. "Oh, you boys." I said. "How you do love to tease." I snatched Lester by the hand and dashed through the door into the cave-like darkness of the Orchid Room.

Chapter 2

The inside of the Orchid Room was about as different from that of the women's bar we'd just come from as a medieval dungeon is from the Johnson Space Center. Here the lights were all red, with a total of about twenty watts worth of bulbs in the whole place, all located in fake lanterns mounted on the wall at shoulder level. The ceiling was supported by a number of pillars in imitation stone that had been posed against so much that most of the textured finish was worn off. There were actually chains hanging from rings on the walls, and, up high enough to be out of the reach of over-enthusiastic patrons, some rusty and obviously unauthentic weapons like maces and swords and spears resided on racks made of spikes driven into the ersatz masonry.

I'd pushed my way inside through the crowd that always seemed to be clogging the entrance of any gay bar, and now I stood gazing around in disbelief. The place was jammed with men, mostly in leather and hardware or in jeans tight enough to cause sterility in a matter of minutes, not that it was going to matter to any of them. I noticed that a lot of patrons had rings of keys dangling from their waists, some on one side and some on the other. I vaguely knew that the keys were some kind of code having to do with S&M, but I didn't have the faintest idea which side was S and which was the other. There were also a few of the regular type of gay men I was used to seeing in Austin, and in this setting they looked like Sunday school superintendents. They also looked mighty good to old Cass Milam, I can tell you. It looked like Lester and I were the only women in the place. Nobody paid the slightest attention to me, which suited me fine. It was hard for me to think of some of these guys as my gay brothers.

"There she is." Lester shook me by the shoulder. "Cass, there she is. See? Over there talking to that ape with the red shirt."

"Where?" I peered around a pillar and strained my eyes to see into the shadowy recess where Lester was pointing.

"There! Right there, can't you see? Jesus, Cass!"

"Okay, okay. Now I see her. You want to go talk to her?"

"You go." Lester was staring at Sharla through the crowd and not looking at me.

I looked at Lester hard. She'd been so anxious to find Sharla, but now she was going to be shy about approaching her. I wondered why. It was hard to believe she was afraid of confronting her, considering the fact that confrontation was what she and Sharla seemed to be best at. Maybe it was the atmosphere in here. It was hard to believe that tough Lester was intimidated.

"I'll get her," I said, and Lester threw me what from her constituted a grateful look. Sort of a sheepish frown. I wove my roundabout way between the displays of macho muscle and edged closer to Sharla and the guy she was talking to.

He was a tall fellow in black jeans and a red satin shirt, all as tight as a second skin. He had no keys at his belt, but the belt itself was about four inches wide and dotted with metal studs. He had high leather boots on that came nearly up to his knees, with the pants stuffed inside them. I wondered how much talcum powder he had to slather all over his body to slide himself into that outfit. His black hair was combed forward and up from the back of his neck, no doubt held by mousse or something. He had a little moustache, too, that looked a bit too small to make the best effect. I suspected he was just in the process of growing it. Neither he nor Sharla saw me approach. I came up beside them and said, "Sharla, fancy meeting you here."

Sharla favored me with a glance of distaste, but the guy she was talking to nearly jumped out of his skin. I guess he thought the place was being invaded by women or something. He looked at his boots and muttered something, and Sharla said, "Cass, why do you always have to sneak up on people when they're having private conversations?"

"Sorry, Sharla. I'll have the butler announce me next time." I looked up, way up, at the red-shirted guy, who seemed to have recovered somewhat from the shock of my arrival and was now grinning like a friendly sheepdog, though still standing half-turned away from me with his face in the shadows. God, were all the men in this place basketball players or something? It seemed like every one of them I actually talked to was six-foot-seven. Sharla, who was about Lester's height, looked like a midget beside this one.

"Very funny, Cass. I suppose Lester sent you? Is she here?" Sharla started bobbing back and forth, trying to see through the crowd in the direction I'd come from.

"She's over there somewhere. She got worried when she didn't know what had happened to you."

"I *told* Jacko." She heaved a theatrical sigh. "Okay. Let's go." She smiled at her male friend "Nice to have seen you."

"Nice to see you," he muttered, still looking at his black-booted toes. "See you." I led Sharla back through the crush to where Lester was still standing, looking angry and a little scared all by herself. She turned as we got to her and headed for the front door without a word, and we followed her out of the Orchid Room and into the crisp October night. I figured the foray into the world of keys and leather had cost me just about a dollar a minute. The guy at the door called out,"Good night, ladies," in a jovial and rumbling bass, and burst into laughter.

Neither Lester nor Sharla seemed inclined to talk as we headed down the block and back toward the other bar, and I didn't much want to get things stirred up by trying to make conversation. We walked in silence, three abreast, our footsteps making a syncopated rhythm on the pavement. But I hate an atmosphere of silent anger; I keep waiting for the bomb to go off, and it gets to me. Finally I said, "Who was the guy in the red shirt, Sharla?"

"Nobody," she snapped, so sharply it made me think there must be something about him she didn't want Lester or me to know.

"I thought it might be a friend of your brother's or something."

"No. Just some guy," she insisted. "He was quite nice to take time to talk to me and tell me about the bar and the men who go there. I thought it was all very interesting."

"Yeah, it was interesting, all right. So your brother told you about that place? Is he into the leather scene?"

"Cass, my brother's business is his own. I'm not going to discuss his lifestyle with someone who doesn't even know him. I'm sure you understand."

"Oh, certainly." I shut up. That sort of thing was why Sharla was not one of my favorite people. She was sure she was way better than me. Besides, I don't think she'd ever forgiven me for being lovers with Lisa—not, I believed, that Sharla really wanted Lisa herself. She just thought Lisa, who has a master's degree and is from a little more moneyed family than mine, was throwing herself away on a menial laborer like me, even if I do own my own landscaping and mowing business. So now we walked along in even more hostile silence than before, and I was willing to leave it at that.

Then, just before we got back to the bar where we'd left our friends, Lester suddenly said, "You think you're such a big shot!"

"What?" Sharla was startled.

Lester stopped and swung in front of Sharla and we

all halted suddenly and awkwardly in the middle of the sidewalk.

"You're always high-hatting somebody, you know it?"

"Lester, really. Not on the street—"

"Yeah, 'really.' I'll talk to you whenever I want to. I've just about had enough of you, you know? First you run out on me and then Cass goes out of her way to help me find you and you give her shit for it, Well, you owe her an apology, Sharla, so let's hear it."

Sharla was getting red in the face. "Lester, that's the most . . . the most childish way of looking at things I ever heard of."

I took hold of Sharla's arm and said, "Now, listen, I'm not offended or anything, so let's just forget all this. . . ." But Sharla jerked violently away from my touch as if I'd been a leper, while Lester was saying, "Childish? You fucking better take that back, Sharla Doyle!"

"Now, Lester, just calm down," I said.

"Calm down, hell!" Her voice was getting pretty loud. "I'll calm down when she apologizes. She's the one that started all this shit." By this time Lester was standing in front of Sharla with her legs braced and her chest stuck out, looking just like an angry bantam rooster, while Sharla was affecting bored indifference to a degree that made even me want to hit her.

"I'll see you both later," Sharla said, and she brushed contemptuously past Lester and darted into the bar. Lester whirled and took a step after her, but I grabbed her and got a good grip on both her shoulders.

"Easy, babe," I told her. "Lets walk a little." I tucked my arm firmly into hers and guided her past the door of the bar and on down the block a ways. She didn't resist except right at first. Then she followed along docilely enough, though turning her head from time to time to look back at the door through which Sharla had disappeared. By the time we were halfway to the corner she even quit doing that and just trudged along gloomily.

"Thanks for sticking up for me," I said when I judged it was safe to reopen conversation.

"She's a shithead," Lester replied.

"Well, she just has a good opinion of herself, I guess."

"Hah! *That's* an understatement!"

"Well, you know she was interested in Lisa a while back, too. I think that has something to do with it."

"Who wouldn't be interested in Lisa? That's no excuse."

"There I have to agree with you. Lisa's something, isn't she?"

"Yeah. Lucky you. Cass?"

"Yeah?"

"Do you think I'm childish?" She said it so timidly I'd have hardly believed it could be Lester talking.

"Childish, no. Hot-headed, yes. I think that's what gets to Sharla."

"She's a shithead. A gold-plated shithead."

We got to the corner and waited for the walk signal. It came on, and we crossed the practically deserted street and entered the shadows of the trees that lined the street between the curb and the sidewalk. I withdrew my arm from the crook of Lester's elbow and put it around her waist instead, and she put hers around me. I was feeling a lot of sympathy for this young butch who was trying to get along with the difficult Sharla. I wondered if I'd have done as well when I was her age. I was pretty hot-headed myself, twenty years ago.

"We probably look like a couple of perverts," Lester said, but she kept her arm around me.

"Fuck the world's opinions, anyway," I said to cheer her up. I was rewarded with a reluctant smile and a little tightening of her arm at my waist. I squeezed her back, and we walked like that for nearly another block before we turned back. We didn't talk any more, but before we went in to join the others, Lester socked me on the arm and said, "Thanks, Cass. You're all right."

"You are too," I said, and we dived back into the brightly lit roar of the bar.

Lisa, Jacko and Tina were at our table, Kelly and Elkhorn were dancing madly amid the throng, and Sharla was nowhere to be seen. Lester said nothing about it.

"Where's Sharla?" I said to Lisa.

"She called a cab and went to her brother's."

"Oh. Is she planning to get back with us, or not?"

"No. She said she'll go back on her own." Lisa looked at Lester, who was listening to us but watching the dancers. I raised my eyebrows and shrugged.

One record ended and the next one started, one with a deep, sexy beat you couldn't help moving to. Lester reached a decision and jerked around to face Lisa. "You wanta dance?" she said.

"Sure!"

They got up and Lester led my beautiful lover onto the dance floor. I grinned at them and settled down to drink a well-earned beer, relieved the crisis was over. I didn't know I'd seen Sharla for the last time.

Chapter 3

By the middle of the next week the weather had settled into a classic late October pattern of cool mornings, warm, lazy afternoons, and chilly nights that made even tough old me think of lighting the heaters. I didn't, of course. The only way I can adjust to the changing seasons is to avoid insulating myself from them too much right at first. Still, I was glad enough of a quilt on the bed at night.

This Wednesday I was alone except for my two cats, Pamela and Chip, and my Chesapeake Bay Retriever, Ronson, who was in the back yard. Lisa was working the four-to-midnight shift at the plastics plant that provided her a living until some kind of job might come along that would let her use her social work degree, although sometimes I wondered how enthusiastic she really was about working in her professional field. She seemed pretty happy in what she was doing, except for the money.

I'd gone to bed early and read a little of a not-very-interesting mystery I'd gotten from the library, then packed it in and slept. These cool nights were good for sleeping.

I was dreaming something I don't remember now, something confusing with a lot of noise in it, and when I woke up the noise seemed to go on. I forced myself to consciousness and listened in the darkness, and then it came again, a fast, hard knocking at the front door and a voice calling, "Cass! Cass!" in a kind of whispered yell. I dragged out of bed and stumbled through the hall and the living room to the front door. I pulled the window curtain aside and looked out, turning on the porch light as I did. It flashed blindingly and burned out. I peered into the darkness and called, "Who is it?"

"Cass! It's me, Lester. Open up, for god's sake!"

I opened the door and Lester snatched the screen open and lunged inside, practically running me down. I caught her by the arms and said, "Take it easy, babe. What is it?"

She stood stiff in my grip and didn't say anything.

"Lester?"

"Sharla got killed."

"What!"

"You heard me, goddammit, Cass. I said she got killed."

"My god, Lester. How—?" I let go of her arms and went to turn on the floor lamp by the couch. Blinking in its light, I looked back and saw Lester still standing where I'd left her, eyes focused on nothing. She looked like she must be in shock. I stepped back to her and guided her to the couch and sat her down. She didn't resist, just let me do it. I sat beside her, turned so I could face her. "Lester, what happened?"

"Car wreck." Her voice was rough.

"Where? How?"

"She went off 2222."

"Went off . . . ?"

"Into the lake. Off one of those curves."

"Oh god, Lester." I put my hand on her knee.

"They called from the hospital. I went down there."

"Oh, Lester. Did you get to see her? Was she . . . ?"

"She was dead by the time I got there. I had the battery out of my fucking bike to charge it and kicked it about a hundred times before I remembered the sonofabitch was gone, and then I dropped one of the terminal nuts in the gravel and couldn't find it, so by the time I got there. . . ." She stared at the far wall, rigid. I tightened my fingers on her knee. "She was unconscious, anyway. They never did get her to breathe again, they said. A guy saw her go off and climbed down the cliff and got her out, but. . . ." she turned anguished eyes on me at last.

"They said she was really dead before he got her out. So I couldn't have got there in time, anyway. That's what they said."

"God, Lester. God, I'm sorry."

Lester went back to staring straight ahead, but tears were finally running down her cheeks. I reached for her and turned her toward me, and at last she wrapped her arms around me and put her head down against me and cried. I let her cry a while, and I cried, too, for Sharla's death and for Lester faced with this so young, and for all who ever died or ever will, I guess. In a few minutes she pushed herself away and sniffled loudly and swiped at her nose with her hand. I went and got her something to blow her nose on and turned on the light in the kitchen and put on water for coffee. Lester followed me into the kitchen and sat at the table while the water boiled and the coffee dripped. I didn't know what to say, so I didn't say much, and she didn't say a word.

I poured her a cup of coffee and got out sugar and cream for her and gave her a spoon.

"You'd better fix that the way you like it," I told her. She stirred in a couple of spoons of sugar and some cream and sipped.

"Good coffee," she said.

"Thanks." I ran some cold water from the faucet into my cup to make mine cool enough for me to drink and joined her at the table.

"Cass?"

"Yeah?"

"I don't want to go home."

"I'm not about to let you. You stay here."

She smiled a little. "Okay."

"Good."

"I . . . Cass, you didn't hate her, did you?"

"No. I didn't. You know we didn't get along the best, but I didn't hate her."

"I didn't think you did." She sipped some more of her coffee, and I drank a swallow or two of mine.

"She was just letting me stay there until I got a place of my own, you know."

"No, I didn't know that."

"She hated loving me."

"What do you mean?"

"She hated it, that's all. I was too butch for her."

And too young, I thought but didn't say.

"But she loved me anyway. Didn't she?" Her voice threatened to break, but she controlled it. "Don't you think she must have?" She looked at me imploringly.

"Sure. She had you living there, didn't she, and I don't think she'd have done that if she hadn't cared about you."

Lester nodded. "That's what I thought." She drank the rest of her coffee in two gulps and banged down the cup on the table. "Let's go to bed," she said.

I followed her into the bedroom, letting her take over in my house if it made her feel better, and crawled into bed while she took off her shirt and pants. Her hands went to the fastenings of her bra and I saw her hesitate, glancing at me.

"There's a tee shirt in the second drawer you can sleep in," I said. She opened the drawer without a word and got out a cotton tee shirt and pulled it over her head, snaking the bra out from under it by contorting her arms. "Get the light, will you?" I said, and she flipped off the switch and got into bed beside me in the dark.

"Cass," she said after squirming around a little and pulling up the quilt against the chill, "I don't understand what she was doing out there,"

"Out on 2222, you mean?"

"Yeah. She didn't tell me where she was going, but I thought she was going out with somebody, or something."

"Wasn't she alone in the car?"

"Yeah. that's what they said."

"Would there be any reason for her to be out that way?"

"No."

"Did she say anything at all about where she was going?"

"No. She just left. We haven't been talking that much."

"Then what made you think she was seeing somebody?"

"Different stuff. And she put on a new blouse." Lester sighed and turned on her side, presenting her back to me. "I'm going to sleep," she said.

"Okay. If you need anything, wake me, Lester."

She grunted, then lay silent. I settled myself to sleep and was finally beginning to drift off after firmly shutting my mind to speculation about Sharla's death and morbid thoughts in general, a skill I'd had to cultivate during the last year, when Lester said tentatively, "Cass?"

"Hmm?"

She didn't say anything else, and in a minute I moved over and put my arm around her. She grabbed my hand like a drowning man, and I held her until, without meaning to, I slept.

Chapter 4

I woke up before the alarm went off at five-thirty and shut it off before it could wake Lester. She was sleeping in the fetal position, knees drawn up, hugging herself with both arms. I could see her outline clearly under the covers, which she'd pulled up so far that only the top half of her head showed above them on the pillow. Seeing her cottony-white hair there was a little shock when I first opened my eyes, I was so used to seeing Lisa's dark head next to mine in the mornings. Not that Lisa spent every night with me, by any means. But she was the only woman I'd been sleeping with for over a year now. It had been a long time since I'd woken up beside a stranger.

I got out of bed carefully and tiptoed into the bathroom. Pamela and Chip, who had been offended by the presence of Lester in their bed, came in from the living room where they'd slept on the couch and began to make their wishes known concerning breakfast. I went into the kitchen and gave them some chow before I did anything else.

The newspaper was lying in the grass of the front yard soaking up the dew, and I went to get it barefooted. It wouldn't be long before I'd have to yield to the season and put shoes on before I went out; as it was, my feet nearly froze when the dew got on them. I hurried in and put on a pair of socks before I even heated last night's coffee. Lester was still sleeping like a log.

The paper didn't have anything about Sharla's accident of course, since it happened so late last night. I wished it had. The whole thing would have seemed like a dream to me except for the fact of Lester in my bed. I wanted to know what exactly had happened and why Sharla was out on 2222 alone, and why she ran off the road at all. I wouldn't have pictured her as a careless or unskilled driver, no matter what I might have thought about her personality as it concerned me. When I thought about it, though, I wouldn't have ever expected her to get tied up with Lester, either. Maybe that showed a kind of recklessness in itself, although I could see that Lester had her charms. Really, I guess I was feeling sort of mother-hennish about Lester. You didn't see too many young butches like her around any more, not like when I was that age. Everybody these days seem to have grown up on feminism and its accompanying femininity. Lester's was a type I liked and missed, and being with her was kind of like stepping back twenty years.

I closed the bedroom door so I wouldn't wake Lester and dialed Lisa's number from the phone in the hall. She answered, sleepy-voiced, and I told her in quiet tones what had happened. "I'll be over there in twenty minutes," she said.

She was, too. I just had time to get breakfast on the table when she walked in the back door. We sat down together and talked across our bacon, eggs, and grits. Watching Lisa scarf down a big helping of grits pleased me; she was a California girl, and before she met me she would never have considered eating this Southern delicacy. In fact, there were several things Lisa probably wouldn't have considered before she met me.

"I can't believe Sharla just ran off a cliff, Cass," Lisa said. "I've ridden with her a bunch of times and she's always been a good, careful driver."

"Maybe she was drunk. We know she did get drunk sometimes."

Lisa cut her eyes at me and said, "*De mortuis nil nisi bonum*, babe."

"Oh, come on."

"That means—"

"I know what it means. My mother used to say it all the time. 'Don't knock somebody who's dead.' Bullshit. She also used to say, 'If you can't say something nice—' "

Lisa joined me, and we finished in unison, "Don't say anything at all!"

"But seriously, Cass, she wasn't really likely to get drunk. I really only saw her drunk that one time, and I don't think she was too bad off, even then."

"You wouldn't remember too much about it, though, would you?"

It was her turn to say, "Oh, come on." Sharla had gotten Lisa drunk and put the make on her when Lisa and I had first started seeing each other, and Kelly and Elkhorn had had to rescue her and drag her out of the bar. It wasn't one of my fondest memories, even now. Lisa's, either. She's not a big drinker.

"Anyway, maybe something went wrong with her car. That old VW never seemed ultra-reliable to me."

Lisa shook her head. "It didn't always start, true, but I do know Sharla was safety conscious. In fact, I remember she had it in the shop for a brake job just at the first of the summer, so it couldn't have been that the brakes went out, I'd think."

"Well, it *could* . . . But what about the tires? Were they slick or anything? Or she could have had a blowout, I guess. Or the steering could have gone out. . . . I'd sure like to see her car."

Lisa frowned. "Cass, the police will look it over, you know. They'll find out what caused it. If she was drunk, they'll find that, and if there was something the matter with her car, they'll find that, too."

"Okay. But what do you bet the paper never says a word about it?" I got up and started clearing the table, and Lisa ran water in the sink to wash up. We'd just about got the dishes done when Cheryll, my employee, came to the back door, knocked, and came on in.

"Cheryll," Lisa said, "did you hear about Sharla?" She was telling her what had happened as I went to get dressed.

In the bedroom Lester had rolled onto her back and was sleeping with a frown on her face. I moved around as quietly as I could, getting my clothes out of the closet and gathering up my keys, billfold, knife, and pocket change, but when I glanced at her again, she was watching me out of half-open eyes. "I'm awake," she said.

"You don't have to get up," I told her. "I'm going to have to go to work, but Lisa's here, and she doesn't have to be at work till four this afternoon, so she'll be around."

Lester sat up and swung her feet off the bed. "I'm getting up," she said.

"Okay. Lisa'll fix you some breakfast."

"I'm not hungry."

"Okay, but there'll be plenty if you want something."

"Okay." She went into the bathroom and I finished dressing. I'd just laced up my boots when Lester came back and picked up her jeans and started getting into them.

"Who's out there?" she wanted to know.

"Besides Lisa? Just Cheryll. I don't know if you know her. She works with me."

"Scrawny fluff with earrings down to her boobs?"

"Well, not quite *that* long, maybe, but yeah, she does tend toward dangly ones."

"Yeah, I know who she is. So she works for you? I guess that's where she gets those ropy arms."

"You seem to have observed her closely, Lester."

"I don't miss much when it comes to women." She looked over at me. "I bet you don't either."

"That'd be telling." I clapped her on the shoulder as I opened the door. "Come on out to the kitchen and let Lisa fix you something to eat. I've got to get going."

I went back to where Lisa and Cheryl were sitting at the kitchen table drinking coffee. "We've got a lot of ryegrass to put in this morning," I told Cheryll, "so let's get out there. This is Lester," I added as I noticed my guest hanging back in the door to the hall.

"Yeah, I know you," Lester said, as Cheryll said, "Hi, Lester."

"I'm sorry about Sharla, Lester," Cheryll went on. "I didn't know her well, but she seemed nice."

"Uh. Any coffee left?"

"Sure," Lisa said. "Here. What do you take in it?"

"Nothing."

Lisa handed her the cup of black coffee. Lester sat down at the table with it and stared at it. I watched her curiously. Last night she'd put a whole bunch of sugar and cream in it, but this morning, nothing. Maybe she liked it different at different times of the day. Cheryll and I went out to hook up the trailer with the tiller on it and went to work.

The yard we needed to seed with ryegrass for the winter was a big, rolling one in north Austin. The house was new, and no permanent grass was established at all. There was just the reddish sandy loam the contractors had spread about four inches deep, probably over the construction rubble if this place was typical.

At eleven we stopped for lunch. I'd gotten the tilling done, just a shallow scratching job to give the seeds a place to get in, and Cheryll was right behind me with the spreader. We didn't have but another hour on this place, including loading up the equipment.

We sat on the tailgate of the truck and unpacked our lunches. I had a couple of sandwiches I'd made the night before and stuck in the refrigerator, plus a candy bar and a sack of Fritos. Cheryll had three sandwiches, some dip, chips, an apple, and a fried pie. We drank coffee out of thermoses, munching and sipping in the contented silence that hard workers know how to share. When we were starting to slow down toward the end of the meal, Cheryll said, "So what was Lester doing at your place? I've never heard you mention her before."

"I guess she just needed someplace to come, and I was handy. She and I just started getting to know each other last weekend."

"In Houston? That's right, you said something about Sharla's having a fight with her lover down there, but I didn't know who the lover was, or if you said, I didn't pay any attention. I've seen Lester around at the bar and all, but I don't know her."

"Yeah, she's at the bar all the time, from what I gather."

"What's her real name?"

"Celeste, somebody told me."

Cheryll giggled. "Lester does suit her a little better, doesn't it? Is she from Austin?"

"Yeah. Her parents live here. In fact, she just moved out of their house when she started staying with Sharla."

"Hm. So what's she going to do now, move back home?"

"I don't know. I didn't ask her. It seemed a little early in the game to start talking about practicalities last night, and then this morning I hardly got to talk to her before I had to rush off. I don't know why she can't stay where she is, if the rent's paid up."

"You mean at Sharla's, or with you?"

"Good god, at Sharla's, of course!" Cheryll was watching me with amusement. "It never occurred to me that she'd stay at my place. But, now that you mention it, I guess it would be kind of hard on her to go back there alone. I guess I'll have to ask her to stay a while— maybe."

Cheryll wadded up her sandwich wrappers and stuffed them back in her lunch sack. "A roommate might do you good, Cass. Rub some of the sharp corners off of you."

"Lisa's done enough of that already, thank you."

Cheryll laughed.

"Lester thinks Sharla had gone out with somebody last night," I said, changing to a less uncomfortable subject. "It's a mystery what she was doing out that way, apparently."

"Seeing a new sweetie, you mean? I never thought Lester was Sharla's type."

"I guess. Lester doesn't seem to know who it was, though. If it was anybody. Maybe she just went out to get away from Lester. I imagine she's not the easiest person to live with."

"Too young."

"Way too young, especially for Sharla, I'd have thought. Too butch, is what Lester says. I can believe that, too."

"They don't know how she ran off the road, though? Lisa said she was alone in the car."

"If they know, it wasn't made public."

"Weird." Cheryll pitched her lunch sack into the back of the truck, and I did the same with mine.

When we got back to my house on Hank Street it was nearly five o'clock. Cheryll hopped in her car and took off, and I backed the truck into the driveway and unhooked the trailer, eagerly supervised through the chain-link gate by Ronson. I'd have to have a ball game with him this afternoon, just as soon as I'd showered and got a beer and read my mail. It was good to get to the house and not see either Lisa's car or Lester's motorcycle. I do like my privacy.

After I'd greeted Ronson with a little roughhousing, I let myself in the kitchen door and savored the silence. I love coming home. I got a Shiner beer out of the icebox and unscrewed the top on my way to the bathroom. I stripped off my clothes, very dusty from the morning's dry tilling, took a delicious swallow of beer, and stepped into the shower.

Minutes later, clean and damp, I picked up the beer again and strolled naked into the bedroom to get into some clean, non-working clothes. I went through the door and stopped dead. On the bed were three alien laundry bags, stuffed full, and on my dresser, taking up nearly the whole top, was a huge portable radio-cassette player with dual speakers. Apparently Lester had moved in.

Chapter 5

A car door slammed in the driveway. A glance out the front window showed me Lisa and Lester pulling some more stuff out of Lisa's car. There were some clothes on hangers, Lester's motorcycle jacket noticeable among them, and there were at least two cardboard boxes, too. I finished putting on my clothes and went to open the front door for them.

Lisa was already nearly to the front porch, straining under the load of a big Jack Daniels box which obviously contained something heavy. I opened the screen for her and she eased her burden through the door, stepping carefully over the sill, and set the box down by the couch. Lester was right behind her with the clothes on hangers.

"There's probably room for most of those in the hall closet, Lester," I told her.

She said, "Okay," and vanished in that direction. Lisa gave me a look that combined resignation with a trace of guilt, as well she might. I doubted that moving in lock, stock, and barrel, had been entirely Lester's idea, and even if it had, she couldn't have done it on her motorcycle.

"There's another box in the car," Lisa said, and I followed her out to get it. At the car we stopped, and she gave me a worried smile. "Is it okay? Just for a little while?"

"I guess it better be. It's done, anyway."

"I told her if you hated the idea too much, she could always stay with me."

"Hell. I've got a big picture of that."

"Well, it'd be okay, if you can't stand it with her here. I know you like your privacy, Cass, but she really needed a place to go, and she asked me what I thought you'd think about her staying with you for a week or two—"

"A week or two! The world could end in a week or two. The sun could go nova in a week or two. The polar ice cap could melt and flood Austin in a week or two. I could lose my mind in a week or two and you'd have to take me to the State Hospital gibbering and squeaking in a week or two." She was looking genuinely unhappy by now, and I could see she was regretting extending this invitation to Lester for me.

"I don't mind having her at my place, Cass. Really I don't. I'll just tell her that's what we'll do."

She looked so distressed at that prospect that I had to laugh at her. I hugged her and told her, "You'll do no such thing, babe. I don't mind having her around. I'll probably enjoy the company for a change. Maybe she'll let me go cruise the Drag on her motorcycle. Look over the college chicks. Hot times, babe. You only live once."

She pushed me away, grinning. "Is it really okay?"

"Yep. It's okay. Only let me ask you this: did you really tell her she could stay with you?"

"Yes, I did, but she said she'd like to stay here, if you wouldn't hate it too much."

"Even baby butches love Mama Milam."

Lester was taking her time hanging up those clothes. I glanced at the bedroom window, the nearest one to where we were standing, and caught a glimpse of movement. She'd been watching to see how I was receiving the news of her semi-permanent installation in my until-now solitary quarters. I slid the last cardboard box, this one advertising Dewar's White Label, out of the back seat of Lisa's Toyota and lugged it into the house. Lester was there to open the screen for me.

"So we're going to be housemates," I said to her. "I hope you can stand it."

"Fine." She took the box from me and stood looking around

"What's in it?"

"Just old stuff."

"Can you get it in the bottom of the hall closet?"

She turned and marched off. At least Lester wasn't likely to talk my arm off. I went into the kitchen, picking up the beer I'd set down on the coffee table, and Lisa came with me.

"It was awful at Sharla's," she said. She sat down at the kitchen table and shook her head when I offered her a beer. I put it back in the icebox, and she said, "On second thought, I guess I do want one."

I gave it to her. "How was it awful?" I asked.

"Her parents and about a dozen relatives were there, including grandparents and cousins and I don't know what all. They treated Lester like a piece of shit—Sharla's father's term, not mine—and refused to let her get her things out of the apartment."

"Jesus."

"No kidding. So I tried to reason with them."

"Good luck."

"Yeah. And her mother, Sharla's, threatened to call the cops and have us arrested for trespassing."

"Jesus!"

"Oh, yes. Lester and I were some of the sick perverts that had corrupted their daughter, who is now, get this, who is now better off dead than she was living the sinful and sick kind of life we depraved lesbos had seduced her into." She took a long drink of her beer.

"Christ! What the fuck did you say?"

"I said Lester could produce a rent receipt made out to her, not Sharla, and that they were the ones trespassing, and I told them I'd call the cops myself if they didn't get out of there in five minutes, that Lester was Sharla's lover, which meant Sharla had chosen Lester over them and that I could certainly see why, and if they wanted all the facts of the case paraded in the *American-Statesman*, all they had to do was give me even one more word of hassle and I was calling a dyke reporter I knew who'd be very happy to get such a hot human interest story."

"Great! Did it work?"

"Well, they let us get all Lester's stuff out anyway."

"Good for you!"

"We also got Sharla's lesbian books and all her copies of *Lesbian Connection* and *Common Lives*, and her silver labyris necklace and her amethyst crystals and a bunch of stuff like that. That's what's in the boxes."

"Good thinking. That's great that you thought of getting all that."

"It was Lester's idea."

Lester came in just then and sat down with us at the table. "You want a beer, Lester?" I said, and she nodded. I got her one and she twisted the top off of it effortlessly. I always at least make a face, since the little flutes on the side of the cap hurt my hand. "Lisa was telling me about what happened today. What a pile of shit."

"Yeah."

"That was good thinking, to get all the dyke stuff out of there."

Lester drank from her beer.

"Did you really have a rent receipt?"

"No. I was saving up for a place of my own."

"Oh, yeah, you told me that last night, didn't you. Well, it worked, anyway. Too bad we don't know some dyke reporters, isn't it? We could use an in with the paper sometimes."

"I was proud of myself for thinking of that one," said Lisa, and Lester looked up and smiled at her in a way that made me suddenly glad that she was staying with me instead of sharing a bed with Lisa. I could vividly picture this good-looking little ultra-butch winning Lisa's sympathy, if not her heart, and I was virtually certain what that would lead to. I didn't want it to, not at all.

"Where's your motorcycle?" I asked Lester to distract her gaze from Lisa.

"Shop."

"In the shop? What's wrong with it?"

"Damn alternator's fucked up or something. The battery keeps running down."

"Oh. When will they have it fixed?"

"I don't know. They said to call them in a couple of days." She gulped her beer. "I just hope it doesn't cost too much."

"Yeah. I meant to ask you, where do you work? I don't even know what you do."

Lester frowned, a common expression of hers. "I was working for HEB, but I quit."

"Why?"

"The dumb prick kept scheduling me for stupid hours, that's why. I told him I wasn't gonna work nights and not get to see my friends, and he said I could do it or quit. So I quit."

"Oh."

"But I'm looking for something else, so you don't need to worry about me paying my way, 'cause I have some money saved up." She scowled at me imploringly, and I had to laugh.

"What's so funny?" she demanded to know.

"Just the idea of your thinking I was expecting you to pay to stay here, that's all. If you can spring for some food and beer every now and then, I can't see that it'll cost me any more to run the house with you than without you."

"I want to pay my own way."

"You will. Just help out around the place some, and we'll come out even." I reached across the table and hit her on the arm with my fist. "You can bring me breakfast in bed."

She looked a little startled.

"And polish my shoes. I've always wanted somebody to polish my shoes. And mow the lawn. If there's one thing I hate, it's outdoor work."

She stared at me for a few seconds, and then a slow grin spread across her face.

"And, let me see," I went on. "What else would I let you do? Hmm. These floors could stand a good waxing. You can do that tonight. I use paste wax. It's easy. You just get down on your hands and knees with a rag and wipe it on a section at a time, and then you wait for it to dry, and you take another cloth and polish real hard," I illustrated with vigorous rubbing motions on the tabletop, "and then when you're through with the whole floor..."

"Yeah? When I'm through, what?"

"You put on another coat."

"Shit!"

"Sure. You want it to last, don't you?"

She half rose from her chair and grabbed for my throat, and I leaned back, laughing, out of her reach, grabbing her hands. We wrestled across the table while Lisa snatched the beer bottles out of danger and backed out of the way.

Lester and I grappled to a standstill, and Lisa set the beer bottles on the counter. "I don't know about you guys, but I'm starving," she said.

"Me too." I ran over in my mind the inventory of food on hand. I couldn't think of much that would feed the three of us without going to the store until I remembered I'd gotten a package of spaghetti and a jar of sauce last week to put on the top shelf for emergencies just like this. I suggested that, and Lester and Lisa agreed with alacrity. I stretched up to get the food down from the cabinet while Lisa rummaged through the bottom cabinet where I keep my pans and came up with the big, two-handled aluminum pot.

"Lester, put some water on to boil," she said, opening the jar of sauce and emptying it into a smaller pan. To me she said, "Do you have parmesan cheese?"

"Might have." I opened the refrigerator and moved a few things around so I could see to the back of the shelves. "No," I concluded. "But I'll run get some. Anybody want to come?"

"I'm staying here to put on the spaghetti," Lisa said. "Lester, why don't you run with her?"

Lester reached around me and got a bottle of beer out of the refrigerator. "I'll buy some more at the store," she said defensively. Lisa handed me her keys, since her car was parked in the drive behind my truck, and Lester and I set off on our first domestic shopping trip.

Chapter 6

After supper Lester cleared the table and started the water running in the sink to wash the dishes. Lisa went to help her, but she shook her head. "I'll do it. You all go off somewhere and talk or whatever."

We thanked her and adjourned to the living room. I sat on the couch instead of my usual comfortable chair so Lisa could sit next to me, and we snuggled close in the chilly evening air.

"When are you going to light your heaters?" Lisa wriggled against my shoulder, hugging herself with both arms.

"Oh, come on, babe, it's not near cold enough yet."

"It's cold enough for me. Don't you freeze at night?"

I frowned at her thoughtfully. "Well, now that you mention it, I have been a little cool lately. But don't worry about me. I won't be any more." I broke into a half-whispered snatch of the World War II song the Women Air Service Pilots used to sing: "I've got a big electric fan to keep me cool while I eat, and a tall, handsome man to keep me warm while I sleep. . . ."

Lisa said, "Oh, Cass!" and pushed away from me, but I grabbed her and pulled her back.

"You should have thought about that sooner, shouldn't you? Where'd you think she was going to sleep? On the couch?"

"Yes, as a matter of fact." We kept our voices low.

"She'd be miserably uncomfortable, and anyway, I don't have that many blankets."

"Want to borrow some? I'm sure I can scrape up some extras."

I looked at her and saw she wasn't really kidding. It never occurred to me she'd worry about me sleeping with Lester, who I figured might look on me as maybe a mother or father or brother or something, but certainly not as anything else. Certainly not as a lover. I kissed Lisa to reassure her. "You would never have anything to fear from that quarter," I said. "Don't you know that?"

"But what about when I come over? What are we going to do, all sleep together?"

"Why not?" I grinned. "We might both learn a thing or two from her, who knows?"

Lisa, who is usually gentle as a lamb, hit me on the shoulder hard enough to jar me pretty good.

"Hey, take it easy!" I moved to cuff her in return, but she dodged and started to tickle my ribs. I clamped my arms to my sides to protect myself and at the same time tried to get hold of her hands. "Don't you have any spirit of adventure?" We twisted and squirmed, neither able to pin the other. Lisa's surprisingly strong. "I thought you were liberal-minded. Ow! Watch that!" My ribs were still sensitive from being cracked by a blow from an iron pipe about a year ago. Lisa, afraid she'd hurt me, immediately drew back, and I leapt on her and held her down on her back on the couch.

"No fair! I thought I hurt you!" she yelled.

"Not a chance!" She heaved and struggled under me, but I outweigh her by quite a bit and didn't have much trouble keeping her down. Then she relaxed for a few seconds, but as soon as I started to ease up, she lurched and tried to get her fingers into my ribs again. I tightened down hard, and she finally quit struggling.

"Okay," she said, panting. "You have me. Now what are you going to do with me?"

"Promise not to tickle?"

"Yes."

"You swear?"

"I swear."

From the softening of the look in her eyes, I believed her. I shifted to get some of my weight off of her, and let her arms go. She slipped them around my neck and drew my head down for a kiss which had in it more than just reconciliation. Lisa kisses incredibly well. I moved so I could have a hand free to stroke her, sliding it in a long, slow sweep down the side of her body and then along her thigh almost to the knee, forgetting everything except what we were doing, forgetting entirely about the alien presence of Lester in the house until I heard the soft thump and click of the kitchen door closing.

"Damn!" I said, and scrambled to my feet.

Lisa sat up, straightening her clothes. We smiled ruefully at each other.

"Want to go to my place?"

I hesitated for a moment in an agony of temptation, then shook my head. "No. Not on the first night she's here."

"I guess you're right." She stood up and kissed me lightly on the lips. I gave her a kiss back.

I walked over to the kitchen door and opened it. Lester was sitting at the table writing something with a pencil and a piece of paper that I recognized as coming from the notepad I keep by the phone in the hall.

"Didn't mean to run out on you there," I said.

"Y'all don't bother about me. I'll stay in here," she said without looking up from her writing.

"What're you doing?"

She moved her hand casually to cover what she'd written and looked up with her usual frown. "Nothing. Just making a list." She stared at me intently for a minute, then said, "Is there anything we need from the grocery store tomorrow?"

"Not that I know of, except something to eat. Do you have any preferences? Cravings? Unsatisfied tastes? The world of mealtime is yours for the choosing, as long as we can afford it. I was actually planning to put on a pot of pinto beans to soak tonight, but if that doesn't appeal, think of something else."

"Just beans?"

"Beans and cornbread and collard greens, I thought. I was going to pick up the collards on my way home tomorrow."

"Fine."

"What did you have on your list?" I took a step toward the table and leaned over to see what she'd written, but Lester snatched the paper away and whipped it out of sight under the table. "Okay." I shrugged my shoulders. "Surprise me, then."

Lisa, who'd been watching from the door, said, "Cass, I'm off. I've got to be at work at midnight and I need a nap first."

"Hey, that's right! I thought you were supposed to be working four-to-midnight this week."

"I traded with Louise."

"You'll have a short day tomorrow then, if you get off at eight and have to be back at four."

"No problem. I sleep fast." She gave me a meaningful look. "I've had to learn that, since I got together with you."

I kissed her and walked her to the front door. She called goodbye to Lester and we stepped outside. The night air was decidedly chilly. I was going to have to give in and light my heaters soon. They were stored in the rafters of the garage, and Lester might be persuaded to earn her keep by getting them down tomorrow. I wanted Lisa to feel comfortable in my house — and I wasn't really so tough I didn't need heat, either. Lester probably was.

At the car, Lisa got in and rolled down the window, and I leaned down for a last, quick kiss. "What about the funeral?" I'd meant to ask earlier, but it was hard to talk about Sharla at all with Lester there. She was putting a brave face on it, but she was so short-tempered and abrupt today that I suspected that she was secretly making pretty heavy weather of getting through the sudden death of her lover, even if their relationship hadn't been too solid.

Lisa sighed. "Her family's taking the body back to Dallas and having the funeral there."

"Great. So her friends can't even come, right?"

"Right. I thought of getting some people together and going up there, but it's in the middle of the day, Monday morning, and everybody has to be at work or in class. I asked Lester if she wanted me to take her up there, but she said no."

"I'll bet that's all she said, too."

"Yes. Just 'No,' and that was it. She's not very communicative, is she?"

"I think she's holding back real hard, that's all."

"Maybe so. Maybe you can bring her out a little bit, having her here. She ought to talk about it. It's not good, keeping her emotions locked up the way she's doing."

"I'll see what I can do. But I guess she'll talk when she wants to and not before. She's a stubborn little cuss."

"So's somebody else I could name." She grinned at me.

"Well, maybe Lester and I can talk in bed. You know, get on more intimate terms, you might say."

"Now, Cass...."

"I'll see if I can think of a way to get her real relaxed...."

"Cass, you creep!"

"Yeah. I bet she and I can find a few things in common, now that I think about it. Kind of compare techniques, or something. Just a little demonstration here and there, just to make things clear . . . that ought to loosen her up. Me, too."

Lisa started the car. "Don't be such a meanie to me, Cass. You know very well you're not going to do any such thing, so don't tease me about it."

I leaned in the window and kissed her on the cheek. "Next time," I told her, "maybe you'll think twice about moving somebody in with me without notice." But I said it with a smile.

I watched her until she was out of the driveway and heading down the street, then deliberately turned away just before she got to the corner. I read one time that it's bad luck to watch a ship out of sight, and I wasn't taking any chances with Lisa. Watching a car out of sight might do the same thing, and I wanted her to come back to me safe and sound.

In the kitchen Lester was no longer working on her grocery list but was just sitting at the table with a cup of coffee between her paws. At least her hands reminded me of paws, big and square, fitting nicely with the stocky rest of her. I like the way I look, taller and less compact than Lester, but I wished, looking at her, that I had the sort of unity that she did, the impression she gave that her body was all one piece, solid. People look at me and think, "fat dyke." I looked at Lester and thought, "draft horse" or "power lifter." Maybe I ought to start working out with weights or something. I'd sure like to look more like that.

"Do you work out?" I asked her.

She looked up at me inquiringly.

"With weights or anything?"

"No."

"Oh. I thought maybe you did. You've got that look about you."

"I used to."

"Ah. It shows. I was wishing I looked that good."

"You look okay." I felt this was high praise, coming from Lester.

"Why'd you quit?"

"Sharla hated it. Anyway, I sold my equipment."

"Oh. Well, maybe if I ever get around to doing anything like that, you can show me the ropes."

"Okay." She went back to staring into her coffee cup. Carrying on a conversation with Lester was uphill work. I glanced at the clock; it was nearly eight. I like to get to bed early, and it was getting on toward that time.

"I need to get those beans on to soak," I said, and turned toward the cabinet to get them.

"They're soaking," Lester said. They were in the big pot on the back of the stove.

"Hey, thanks!" I said, and Lester said, "Uh." I took that to mean, "Oh, you're welcome, think nothing of it," or something along those lines.

"I'm about ready to hit the sack," I said. "How about you?"

"I'll be in in a little while." She looked up at me. "Unless you want me to sleep on the couch. I don't mind."

I wondered how much of what Lisa and I had said had been overheard. Not the "tall, handsome man to keep me warm while I sleep" part, I devoutly hoped. I didn't think Lester would take kindly to being kidded that way.

"No, there's room for you in the bed," I said.

"Okay. I'll be in later."

"Fine." I got ready for bed, glancing into the kitchen on the way between bathroom and bedroom, and she was still sitting there the way I'd left her. I went and got under the covers on the far side of the bed next to the windows, leaving room for my new housemate to slip in without having to stumble around in the dark too much, and slept almost instantly. My last thought was that it was kind of nice to have somebody still awake in the house for a change while I was asleep, sort of a homey, safe feeling.

I usually sleep like a log, but I must have been waiting with part of my mind for Lester to come to bed. When she hadn't by two o'clock, I woke up. I could still see the light from the kitchen slanting down the hall, but I didn't hear anything.

"Lester?" I called her name, but got no response. I crawled out of bed, breaking out in goosebumps as the cool air hit my bare skin—in warm weather I sleep in my shorts and a tee shirt—and padded on cold bare feet into the kitchen. Lester was asleep with her head on the table, her upper body sprawled across an array of books and papers. The box they'd come from, one of those she'd brought from Sharla's, was on the floor beside the chair.

"Lester?" I touched her shoulder lightly, and she jerked awake like I'd given her a jolt with a cattle prod.

"Easy, babe!" I'd jumped back a foot and a half. She

glared at me out of half-open eyes and tried to cover the things on the table with her arms.

"Is that Sharla's stuff you're going through?"

"Yeah."

"Are you looking for anything in particular?"

"No."

"Why don't you come to bed. It's getting chilly out here." I was hugging myself by this time to conserve what little warmth I still had and my feet were freezing.

"In a minute." She started gathering up Sharla's papers and dropping them back haphazardly in the box. There were several folders, the kind with pockets to hold loose papers, and a legal pad with what looked like sociology class notes, from the glance I got at it before Lester whisked it away, and there were several spiral notebooks with the abbreviations of U.T. courses on the covers in magic marker. I couldn't imagine what Lester was finding interesting in Sharla's school stuff. I wondered if maybe she just wanted to hold on to Sharla somehow and this was about all she had of her to hold onto. Poor Lester. I waited for her to finish repacking the box, and she hauled it back to the hall closet and trudged into the bathroom without another word. I went back to bed, frozen through, and tried to find the warm place I'd left between the sheets.

In a few minutes Lester came in, undressing in the dark with her back to me so I wouldn't see her breasts in the faint light from the windows and pulling one of my tee shirts over her head. Lester, I was tickled to see, wore men's Jockey shorts just like me.

She got into bed, turned her back to me, and settled in.

"Goodnight, Lester," I said.

"Night."

"Sleep well."

"Uh." She paused a few seconds, then added, "You, too."

It was more cordiality than I'd come to expect. I went to sleep.

Chapter 7

Cheryl and I got through with our work by two o'clock the next afternoon and knocked off early for the weekend. It was Friday, with no Saturday work lined up, which was good in a way and bad in another, and I was looking forward to a rest. It hadn't been the most relaxing week I'd ever spent in my whole life. In the last two days, in fact, my whole pattern of living had been scrambled, what with Sharla's death and Lester's moving in. I could have gone calling on some of my old customers and tried to drum up some late tree-planting business, I guess, but all I wanted was a Shiner beer and some peace and quiet. I headed home.

I got the Shiner out of the refrigerator, and that was as much of my heart's desire as I was going to get, because even from the street I'd been able to hear Lester's radio blaring out rock music from my — or I guess I should be saying "our"— bedroom. I'd found Lester at the kitchen table again, surrounded by stacks of Sharla's class notebooks and folders, with a beer at her right hand and a notepad and pen beside it. I didn't get a chance to see what she'd been writing because, as usual, she covered it up as soon as I walked in the door.

I opened my beer and sat down across the table from Lester, being careful not to look at Sharla's papers. I was afraid that if I did, Lester would knock over the beer in her haste to cover the whole mess with her arms and body to protect it from my prying eyes.

"Hi," I said. I gave her a grin. At least she was doing something, whether it was a secret or not, and not just giving in to grief the way a lot of people would have. Also, I was pleased to have been greeted by the savory smell of beans and collards cooking. It made up, a little, for the detestable music. I like that kind of sound in the bar, but not in my house.

"Hi," she said back. "I'm cooking supper, but it's gonna be a while. How come you're home?"

"Knocked off early." I was beginning to sound just like her, talking in shorthand. "How long till those things get done? They smell great."

"A couple of hours."

"Can you make cornbread, too?"

"Yeah. It's not near time, though." She sipped moodily at her beer, watching me defiantly to be sure that I wasn't spying on her paperwork. The music was interrupted by a string of commercials that was louder and more frenetic than the record had been. I drew a deep breath and held it, willing myself not to get more irritated by the noise than I already was. I wanted a shower and a romp with Ronson in the back yard, and above all, I wanted quiet. I thought of telling Lester to turn the infernal thing off, but she was just a kid who'd lost her lover and maybe the racket was soothing to her or something. I stood up, suddenly remembering something that gave me a surge of hope.

"How many beans did you fix, Lester? The whole package?"

"Yeah. I didn't count 'em. . . ."

I socked her on the arm. "Are there enough for company, is what I meant."

"How much company?"

"Just Jacko. I thought, if it was okay with you, I'd get her to come over for supper. She's off Fridays."

"How come she's off?"

"She works four ten-hour days, Monday through Thursday. So, what do you think?"

Lester shrugged. "Okay with me. I'll make extra cornbread."

I practically skipped to the phone in the hall and dialed Jacko. It rang, and her damn machine said, "Hi! This is Jack—" before she cut in on it. I hate those things, and it seems like everybody's got them.

"Hey, babe," I said, "how about coming for supper with Lester and me?"

"Lester and you?"

"Yeah, she's staying here for a while. What about it?" I didn't want to discuss the situation over the phone where Lester could hear it.

"Well . . . Tina and I are going to the bar later, but, yeah, okay. As long as I get back in time."

"No sweat. I'll come pick you up."

"What? You want to pick me up?"

"Yeah. I'll be right over."

"Why? If I drive over there, I can just leave from there for the bar, but if you come and get me, you'll have to bring me all the way back over—"

"I'm on my way," I said, and hung up. I dashed into the bedroom and grabbed a clean shirt which I threw on over my unwashed body and high-tailed it out to the truck. As I drove off down the block, I could still hear Lester's music, fading slowly behind me. I grinned and started to sing. I sound much better than the radio.

When I got to Jacko's place, I parked the truck and climbed the stairs to her door. I thought of all the times I'd made this climb under circumstances that ranged from the tragic to the comic with a whole lot of in-betweens. Jacko and I had been friends for years and friendly, sometime-lovers ever since we met through a drag queen we both knew. I remember 'Georgia' saying, "I met the nicest dyke," and those were the days when one didn't use that word except among very good friends; it was considered entirely derogatory by most people. I'd pricked up my ears and asked questions, and the next night he'd rounded up Jacko and brought her to the bar to meet me. She was as butch as me and sexy as hell, and neither of us had a lover at the time. We hit it off right away, except for the rather strong disagreement over what women in the bar were attractive. She likes fluffs, the younger and fluffier the better, and I like lesbians who look like lesbians. Jacko thought I was perverted to like these butch types when I was one myself. I thought she was perverted to like women who looked like they couldn't take care of themselves and who were just as likely, it seemed to me, to run off with a man as with her. A lot of them did just that, over the years, and Jacko moaned over her losses and went right back to chasing the same types again. And in between times, when neither of us had anything else going, Jacko would swallow her pride and go to bed with me, even though she was otherwise a complete stone butch who never let a woman make love to her. We were really good in that department, but we weren't in love with each other, so it was just all pleasure and no complications at all. A nice relationship.

Today, though, I had other things on my mind, and when Jacko opened the door, dressed for the bar and with her house keys in her hand, I put my hand on her chest and pushed her back into her apartment.

"Do you love real loud rock and roll?" I said. "Because if you do, we can go straight back to my place and you'll have a ball. Otherwise, we can stay here for a while and let me get my eardrums readjusted."

"What's up?" She went into the kitchen and I followed her. She got a beer out of the icebox and handed it to me. She got a revolting diet soda of some kind for herself.

I told her about Sharla. She'd heard about it by the grapevine but didn't know any more about it than the rest of us did, and I told her about Lisa's inviting Lester to stay in my bachelor abode with me, and about how that was working out so far.

We talked and drank, and it was really good to get away from it all for a while. Jacko is too opinionated about most things to be really restful to talk to, but this time was an exception.

"So you're sleeping with Lester instead of Lisa now, huh?" she said as we finally walked out the door.

"Yes, but sleeping only."

"I thought she'd be a little too butch—even for you."

"Oh, come on, Jacko. It's not just that. She's really an emotional mess right now, or at least I guess she is; she's hiding it pretty hard. And anyway, you know Lisa's who I care about. Besides, I think Lester's about eighteen, for god's sake."

"I don't see anything wrong with that."

"No, I know you don't. But just think how many times you've gotten burned by those young 'uns. No, thank you." I opened the passenger door of the truck for her, and closed it after she got in. "She's kind of cute, though," I said, and we grinned at each other. I knew "cute" was never going to be the word Jacko would apply to a drag butch. But I would.

The house was as quiet as it had always been. No music greeting our ears as Jacko and I got out of the truck and walked up to the back door, only an excited bark from Ronson when he recognized Jacko, a favorite of his. She stopped to tousle his head and fondle his chestnut muzzle while I unlocked the back door. The kitchen table was empty of its load of Sharla's books and papers, and Lester was not to be seen.

"Lester?" I stepped into the hall and could see that the doors to the bathroom and bedroom were both open, so she ought to have heard me if she was home. "Lester, are you there?" I walked into both rooms and glanced into the living room, too, but the house was empty except for Chip and Pamela, curled together on the end of the couch in a mute protest against the October chill that was now lingering even into the sunny afternoons. I'd have to get those heaters out of the garage and light them pretty soon, but it was hard to say goodbye to another summer.

I went back into the kitchen and finally noticed the note Lester had left on the counter, weighted down by a can of peas. "Cass," it said in a bold and surprisingly mature-looking scrawl, "Gone to pick up bike. Will make cornbread when I get back. L."

I got a beer for myself and one for Jacko, paused to check the beans and the collards, simmering over low flames on the stove and sending out an aroma so mouth-watering that I could hardly resist dishing up at once, and went out to the back yard where Jacko had been trapped by Ronson into a ball game.

They made a pleasant picture, the short, round Jacko in her black slacks and black turtleneck with a blue-green brocade vest over it fastened across the front with two gold chains, hurling the bright green tennis ball for the bounding, curly-haired, red-gold dog who leaped higher than Jacko's head to make his catches. I stood close to Jacko and rubbed my arm against her shoulder affectionately.

"Here's a beer, babe," I said. She looked up and smiled as she took it, that smile that lights up her whole face and that's always charmed the socks off of me ever since we met. Ronson, seeing we were through with him, retired to his favorite spot under the hackberry tree with the tennis ball, made newly valuable by Jacko's handling, between his paws. Jacko and I went over to the lawn chairs and sat down.

"So where's Lester?"

"Gone to get her motorcycle. She left a note."

"Where is it?— The motorcycle, not the note."

"In the shop getting the alternator worked on. I wonder how she got over there? I'd have given her a ride if she'd waited. Or let her take the truck. They could have loaded it in the back with the tiller ramp." I thought of Lester behind the wheel of my Chevy truck. She'd look good driving it, I thought. Cheryll, who often drove it on jobs, always looked like she must have borrowed it from her boyfriend.

"Well, at least I don't hear any music."

"True, and you can't imagine how happy that makes me. What is it, Jacko? Am I getting that old? I used to love having the radio on all the time. Now it just seems like an intolerable imposition. I can't *think* with all that ruckus, you know? I don't *want* to be that excited and worked up all the time. And there's Lester, peacefully working away at some project or other with Sharla's papers, and the damn radio going so loud you can hear it halfway up the block." I drank from my beer. "I swear, it makes me feel like a hundred years old."

"Old rocking chair's got you, huh?"

"Yeah." I got up. "I better go check on supper."

I did that and returned. Ronson had his head in Jacko's lap, rolling his eyes ecstatically as she petted him. I had a good idea how he felt.

"I wonder how long she's been gone?" I said. "She ought not to take too long; the place is just over by Ben White."

"If she tried to come back by Ben White, we won't see her for hours in that traffic." Jacko never passes up a chance to get in a dig at conditions in south Austin. She's always considered it a betrayal that I moved south of the river when I bought my house on Hank Street. She hurried on with a change of subject. "What project is that you said she's working on?" She wasn't going to give me a chance to defend my side of town.

"Damned if I know. She was up half the night last night going through all the papers and books she and Lisa rescued from Sharla's parents—" I'd explained to Jacko about the scene at Sharla's on the way over—"and this afternoon when I got in, she was doing a lot of the same thing, as near as I could tell. She's keeping some kind of notes, but she won't let me see them."

"Hm."

I thought for a minute, sipping beer. An idea was forming at the back of my mind. "I wonder if she's trying to find out who Sharla was supposed to be seeing the night she died?" I told her, as nearly as I could remember, what Lester had said that night about thinking Sharla had been going out with somebody.

"What made her think so?"

"Nothing she could tell me, really. I think she said she put on a new outfit or something like that. Nothing concrete, I don't think."

"Surely if she'd been out with somebody, they'd have told somebody about it when Sharla got killed."

"You'd think so, wouldn't you? Unless it was somebody with some reason to hide. Like, say, somebody who had another lover and was seeing Sharla on the side, or something like that."

"I know Lester wasn't satisfied that Sharla would have gone off that cliff like that without any reason. But it said in the paper that she just lost control of the car. Of course, they just had about an inch-long article on it. But wouldn't they have said if she was drunk?"

"They always do, I think."

"Or if something was wrong with the car? So I don't know. Anyway, I don't see what Lester could be looking for in all those boring class notes. And apparently she intends for me never to know, the way she leaps to cover up what she's doing every time I come into the room."

"Why don't you ask her?" Jacko was looking at me quizzically. "Are you afraid she'll bite your head off?"

I laughed. "She is pretty formidable when she's stirred up. But no, I guess I just want her not to think I'm going to be nosing in her business. She's an independent little cuss."

"You really like her, huh, lady."

"Yeah, I do. She's a lot like I used to be." I paused. "I just wish I'd been as much in control of myself back then as she seems to be now. Maybe things would have worked out differently."

"You're thinking of Claudia again?"

I sighed, then grinned at Jacko. "Yeah, and I'll quit it. 'Let the dead past bury its dead.' It's been a long time, babe."

Claudia was my first lover, and we'd been together when I was about Lester's age. I'd had to come to terms with the fact that I'd never found anybody really to replace her and that I wasn't going to at this late date, and

I'd spent the last year getting used to that idea and getting on with my life after a crisis of remembrance that had gotten me down about as far as I could get. Lisa's calm, loving presence had helped a lot, and so had my old friend Jacko. At thirty-nine, I wasn't ready to die yet, so I was having to figure out how I wanted to live, given the real conditions of my life. It had been a rough year.

The rumble of a V-twin engine in the driveway announced Lester's return, just in time, I thought, to make the cornbread she'd promised before we all starved to death. She came strolling back to the gate, looking more relaxed and happy than I'd seen her since she came here, her black and red helmet dangling by its chinstrap from one hand.

"Hey," she said by way of greeting.

"Got your bike back okay?"

"Yeah." Her smile was delightful to see after her constant frown that I'd gotten used to. Obviously her motorcycle meant a lot to her.

It was the first time Jacko had seen Lester since Sharla's death, but she apparently picked up on Lester's rare good humor and didn't mention anything about it. I gave her credit for perceptive judgement.

"You still feel like cooking, or you want me to whip up some cornbread? The beans and greens smell great," I told her.

"I'll do it." The frown reappeared. "I said I would." She vanished through the back door.

I looked at Jacko and shrugged.

"Just a smidgen touchy, would you say?" Jacko grinned.

"Just a mite." I finished my beer and looked at Jacko's to see if she needed another one yet. She didn't, of course. She'll take a couple of hours to drink one. It's a habit she's developed at the bars. Not only does she not get too drunk to pursue her lady of the hour, but she also spends next to no money that way. I like my beer too much to nurse one like that, and I like to get high on it, too. But then, I'm not usually concentrating on a new conquest like Jacko so often is.

The sudden blare of rock music jolted me. Lester was home, okay. I swept up my beer bottle and headed for the kitchen. "Time for another one of these," I told Jacko.

Chapter 8

Friday night at the Hairpin Turn was loud enough, I thought, to suit Lester. The jukebox was pounding out song after song, women were dancing in such a thick crowd it would be hard to tell by looking who was dancing with whom, and every table was taken by the ones who'd gotten there in time to find chairs. Tina, the woman Jacko had been seeing for about a year now, some kind of a record for my lady-killer friend, had grabbed a table and some chairs before we'd gotten there and managed to defend them against all comers, so the four of us had a place to sit.

Lester had tried to stay home and not come with us, but I'd insisted, so she'd come along. I didn't think moping alone would do her any good in the circumstances, and I didn't know but what she might drink a lot of beer and go out riding on her motorcycle. Not a good idea. Also, the thought crossed my mind that if any harm came to her from drinking at my house, I could be in trouble. She wasn't legal drinking age yet.

We sat at our table, Tina drinking a deep red concoction in a tall glass, Jacko presiding over her traditional Scotch and water in which she was letting the ice cubes melt, and Lester and me with bottles of Shiner.

"Tina, what's that you're drinking?" I always asked her, because she was forever coming up with some new drink nobody else had ever heard of. It seemed like she'd start it, and then the next thing you knew, everybody except us diehards who were completely set in our ways would be guzzling the same thing for a while.

"Try a sip." She offered me the glass. I tasted it and found it sort of syrupy but not bad. It had crushed ice in it, and enough vodka to deck a Russian. Tina could hold her liquor.

"What do you call it?"

Tina smiled sweetly at me and gazed into my eyes. "Do you like it? It's a Lesbian Crush. Have one on me."

I laughed. "You're kidding! What's in it?"

"Grenadine, club soda, crushed ice, a little lime juice, and three jiggers of vodka."

"Lord!"

"Want one? It beats that old beer, Cass."

But I was immune to her charms, especially with Jacko sitting right there, an amused but slightly watchful expression on her face. "Thanks, but I'll stick with my old faithful, Tina."

She made a pouting face and then giggled. "Speaking of Lisa, where is she tonight?"

"At work till midnight."

"And then at your place, huh?"

"Well, I don't know...." I cast a quick look at Lester out of the corner of my eye. Lester didn't see it, but Tina did.

"Lester," she said, "I hear you're quite a cook."

"Who says?" Lester switched her attention instantly from the dance floor, where she'd been studying the various couples, to the three of us at the table with her, darting suspicious glances from Tina to Jacko to me.

"Jacko was bragging about your cornbread while we were dancing just now. She said I ought to get your recipe."

"It's nothing." Lester scowled.

"That's not what I heard," Tina said.

"No, it was really good," Jacko joined in. Lester, who was looking more like a thundercloud every minute, didn't say anything.

"So, would you teach me how to make it? Please,

Lester?" Tina assumed her little-girl whine that I hated so much. "You aren't keeping your recipe secret, are you?"

Lester got up and stalked off, the red glow of the bar lighting catching her snowy white hair and turning it pink like cotton candy. You'd have thought she was an albino except that her skin was tanned and her eyes were a blue so deep they looked like sapphires or lapis lazuli. I watched her walk off toward the bar and thought of what a striking couple she and Lisa would make, with Lisa's fair skin and dark hair and eyes of a clear blue, much lighter than Lester's. The picture was aesthetically pleasing but most unsettling to contemplate. Anyway, I told myself, I looked pretty good with Lisa, myself. My hair's about the same color as Ronson's, and my eyes are sort of golden brown. Lisa hadn't complained, anyway.

Jacko reached across and patted Tina's hand. "Never compliment a baby butch on her cooking, sweetheart."

"Oh. Is that it? I didn't realize what was wrong."

"Don't worry about it," I told her. "She's probably proud of the compliment at some level; it just doesn't go with her image, is all."

"And now she'll probably never cook for Cass again," Jacko said, laughing.

"Oh, god," I said. She was probably right.

I danced a few dances with different women I knew, walking around between times and talking to friends and acquaintances at the tables and where they were standing around in groups shouting to each other above the music. I put down a few beers in the process, too, but not enough to feel any more than a pleasant buzz. Lester, who had come back to the table and sat with us for a minute or two now and then, had spent most of the evening doing her own thing, though I had no idea what that involved besides the fact that I noticed her circulating among the women there at least as much as I was doing. It puzzled me fleetingly when I realized that, because I never remembered seeing Lester socializing much before. In fact, she hardly used to talk in the bar except to Sharla and had a reputation for unfriendliness. Now, though, every time I glimpsed her, she was deep in conversation. I shrugged my shoulders and asked an old lover of mine to dance.

About the time I was thinking about going home, Kelley and Elkhorn, whose antics on the dance floor had been keeping me and a lot of other people entertained, dropped into Jacko's and Tina's chairs while I was alone at the table.

"Y'all do a good job out there," I said, gesturing toward the dance floor. I was rewarded with a pair of dazzling, toothy smiles.

"Thanks," they said in unison, and Kelley continued, "I take it that Lester thinks Sharla had some kind of heavy date the night she was killed. Did she, do you know?"

"No, not that I know of." I frowned, remembering what Lester had said the night Sharla died. "But, yeah, I know Lester thinks so. Why? How do you know about it?"

"She's been giving practically everybody in the bar the third degree," Elkhorn said.

"Oh, yeah?"

"Yeah. So we've asked around a little, too."

"And?"

"And nothing. If she was seeing anybody but Lester, nobody knows about it."

"And believe me, *some*body would know about it," Kelley said.

"Well," I said, "I guess she just can't accept the circumstances, you know. She's trying to make some kind of sense of things, or something. This isn't easy on her. Especially with the way Sharla's family treated her when she went to get her stuff."

"Yeah," said Kelley, and Elkhorn said, "We heard about that. How shitty can you get?"

"And the funeral's in Dallas Monday, I guess you know, so nobody's going. At least, I don't suppose Lester's thinking about going up there; she hasn't said anything to me."

"We all ought to go," Elkhorn said. "That'd show them."

"Yeah!" Kelley seized the idea. "We really ought to! What do you say, Cass? We can't let them pretend Sharla wasn't a dyke, can we?"

"Well...." I remembered when these two and some others had come to my rescue before, and I thought of Lester and how much Sharla's death really meant to her, and I thought of all the lesbians who'd died and been taken away from their friends and their lovers and been buried by their families with no acknowledgment of their love for women. "Hell, why not?" I said. "Hell, yes! Let's get it organized." We huddled over the table, writing a list of people each of us should talk to on a page torn out of my pocket notebook. Sharla was going to have a better funeral than her family expected.

Chapter 9

Lester huddled under the quilt with her feet drawn up so high I think her knees were touching her breasts, hugging herself and shivering. I wasn't that cold, but I was a little too cool for absolute comfort. It had cooled off considerably while we'd been at the bar.

"Why don't you put something on your legs?" I asked her. "I've got some pajama pants you could borrow."

"No. I'm fine." Her voice was muffled by the quilt, and with her back to me I could hardly make out her words.

"Well, I'm going to put some on." I swung my feet to the icy floor and hustled across to the dresser. In the bottom drawer I found my favorite flannel pajamas and another pair for Lester, which I tossed onto the bed over the hump in the covers where her knotted body lay. "Try those," I said.

I stripped off my Jockey shorts and tee shirt and pulled on the pajamas. They were cold, but the soft material felt good, and I liked the loose way they hung on me. I slid back under the covers and wriggled a bit, trying to find exactly where I'd left the spot I'd warmed. Lester sighed and threw back the covers on her left side, got up, and examined the pajamas I'd given her. I could see the critical way she looked them over even in the shadowy outline of the tilt of her head. She was probably, I thought, thinking over how she'd look in them. Lester was ever conscious of her image.

I could tell by the tight way she held herself, legs pressed together, upper arms fast against her body, that she was freezing. If it had been lighter, I would have probably been able to see goosebumps. But she took her time and finally laid the suspect garments back on the bed and pulled off her shirt. As she jerked it over her head, I got a silhouetted glimpse of her breasts, looking young and round, nipples erect in the cold. It was a glimpse I knew she didn't want me to have, so I glanced away quickly, smiling in the dark. I heard her stepping out of her shorts and into the pajama pants, and then she hustled back into bed and pulled more than her share of the covers over her.

"Hey," I said, tugging back. "Leave me some."

"Sorry." She relinquished a few inches of sheet and quilt, which I tucked around my freezing butt.

"I guess we need to give up and get the heaters in tomorrow," I said.

"Uh. Where are they?"

"In the garage, up in the rafters."

"I'll get 'em."

"That'd be great. You'll have to climb up and stand on the tractor, so be careful. There's one for the bathroom and a little one for in here and a big, heavy one for the living room. You might need some help getting that one down."

"I'll see about it."

"Okay. Just be careful."

"I won't drop your heaters."

"Just don't drop you. If you break an arm or something, I'll have to let you use my truck to get around town, and I'd have to use your motorcycle, and it's getting a little chilly for biking, it seems to me."

"I'll be careful."

"Seriously, don't you get awfully cold in the winter on that thing? The wind chill must be something fierce."

"Nah. I got a good jacket."

"But what about your hands? And your knees? I bet your knees just about freeze stiff."

"They're okay."

"If you say so. Do you wear long underwear?"

"Don't have any."

"You ought to get some. That's what I wear in the winter, and it really makes a big difference. You ought to try it."

"Maybe."

A long silence followed, and I nearly drifted off to sleep, and then Lester said, "Cass?"

"Yeah?"

"Are all those women really going to Dallas?"

"A lot of them, I think."

"Why?"

I thought for a minute. "A lot of different reasons, I guess. Some, like Lisa and Susan and Lucia, because they were good friends of Sharla's, and some others because they feel like when a lesbian dies, that's kind of a death in the family and you ought to go and show your respect, whether you really knew her well or not. And it's kind of a political act, too, you know? Like marching in the gay pride parade or something. Showing the hets who we are and how we stick together. And that's the kind of thing Sharla would have done too, isn't it?" She was silent. "Why, do you feel uncomfortable about it?"

"I don't care."

"And none of us think you ought to have to be alone then, either, babe."

"Uh."

"These are your friends, too, you know."

"I'm not going."

"What?"

"Fuck it, Cass, why do you always say that? You heard me. I said I'm not going!"

I didn't know what to say. I lay there a minute, confused. I didn't know whether to try to talk her into it or try to find out why she felt that way, or what. It had never occurred to me that she might not go to the funeral if all the rest of us were going.

"I hope you're not upset about the rest of us being there," I finally said.

"No. Do what you want to."

"What will you do while we're gone?"

"Stuff. I don't know. Just leave me the fuck alone about it, okay?"

"Sure, babe."

I waited to see if she was going to say anything else, or if she was seeming like she could sleep. She lay stiffly with her back to me, neither relaxing nor speaking, for quite a while. I wished I'd talked to her before the rest of us started making our plans. I didn't think I could get her to come if her mind was made up, and I didn't much like the idea of her being left in town by herself, either. At any rate, it was a couple of days until Monday, and a lot could happen in a couple of days.

Lester finally shifted impatiently and turned onto her back. "What are you gonna do, just lie there awake all night?" She tried to seem peeved, but I thought I detected a little conciliatory tone in her voice.

"No, I'll sleep, don't worry. How about you?"

"I'm fine."

"Okay."

She had her eyes open, as near as I could tell in the dark, staring at the ceiling. Another minute or so passed, and I closed my eyes but kept listening for her to shift and get comfortable.

Finally she said, "Cass?"

"Yeah?"

"Do you kiss butches?"

"What!"

"Goddammit, Cass, don't *always* say—"

"Okay, sorry, I didn't mean to say 'what' again. Sorry. You just took me by surprise, that's all. How'd the subject come up?"

"I just want to know. Well? Do you?"

I laughed. "That's about all I kiss, as a matter of fact. Why?"

"Lisa's not butch."

"Well, maybe not compared to you or me. But she's no little fluff, either."

"Well, maybe not . . ."

"She's neither one, really, I guess. She's a lesbian-feminist. They're a different animal from butches and fluffs."

"You can say that again." She paused. "Sharla was one, too."

"Yeah, she was."

"I thought she was a fluff at first."

"Yeah?"

"But she wasn't. She was kind of butch in some ways. But I was butcher."

"I expect you were."

"She let me make love to her."

I waited.

"She liked it."

"I'd expect that."

She paused again, but I knew she'd go on. It was obvious she was leading up to something.

"But she wanted me to . . . to let her . . . do stuff to me, too." She shuddered. "I mean, like, she wanted to do all the same things to me that I do, you know?"

I refrained from laughing. Lester obviously had some notions about roles that Sharla had shaken up. "Yeah, I know," I told her.

She turned to face me, staring earnestly into my eyes in the dark. "So I wondered, these butches you kiss, like Jacko? I know you and Jacko go to bed, don't you?"

"Yeah, we do. Or we used to, before Tina latched onto her and before I got involved with Lisa. Yeah."

"I mean . . . you don't let 'em. . . ."

"Let women make love to me? Sure I do."

"Oh."

"I gather you don't?"

"Hell, no!"

"Why not Lester? It's real nice."

"Oh, god. I just *couldn't*! I mean . . ."

"Of course, you do have to give up a little control, if that's what worries you. But not much. You can still call the shots pretty well."

"I'm going to sleep now."

"Okay, babe."

"Night."

"Good night, Lester."

She turned her back again and settled herself to sleep. I wondered if she was afraid of sleeping with me, now that she'd established to her horror that I was not the stone butch she'd hoped I was. I turned my back, too, so I wouldn't accidentally put my arm around her in the night and scare her to death.

Chapter 10

I'd thought a lot could happen in the two days between Friday night and the day of Sharla's funeral, and what did happen was that Lester disappeared.

I don't know what time it was when we'd finally gotten to sleep after our discussion of Sharla's funeral and the proprieties governing what real butches allow in bed, but it was very late for me. I'm a morning person, and going to the bar and staying up late wipes me out. Anyway, I'd slept like a log when I finally had gotten to sleep, and the next thing I knew, it was pale, early morning and some noise had waked me up. Lester wasn't in bed, but I figured she was just in the bathroom or something. I was still drowsy, and I didn't call her to see.

Then I heard a motorcycle start up somewhere, but that didn't really register, either. Anyway, it didn't leave right away, just idled softly for a while. I thought sleepily that I ought to look out the window to be sure that was Lester fooling with her bike and not somebody stealing it, but I drifted off to sleep again instead. The next thing I knew, it was broad open daylight. Chip, my orange striped male cat, was standing on my chest, kneading with iron feet and purring loudly enough to wake the dead.

"Okay, okay," I told him. I pushed him aside and swung my feet out of bed. The floor was cold, and I was glad of the flannel pajamas I'd put on mainly to encourage Lester to do the same. I pulled on a pair of thick socks before I walked into the bathroom and I slipped my moccasins on, too. Lester's pajamas were folded neatly on the top of the dresser beside her monster radio. I certainly didn't have any quarrel with her housekeeping. She was neater than I was.

When I walked into the bathroom, I was astonished. The room was toasty warm. Lester had already gotten the heater out of the garage rafters and hooked it up and lit it. "Well!" I said to Chip and Pamela, who had followed me in to be sure I didn't forget that my main purpose in getting up in the morning was to feed the cats. "Lester's really getting with it this morning, isn't she?" A look at my watch told me it was nearly eight. Late for me to be getting up, but pretty early for most people I knew to be getting work like that done. And she must have been careful to be extra quiet, too. I examined the connections at the heater and the gas jet, and I could see that she'd actually checked them with soapy water just like you're supposed to. I could see the spots where it had dripped on the floor. "Good for you, Lester," I said to my absent friend.

The kitchen was empty of Lester but full of warmth, and the living room was, too. She'd installed the big heater in the living room and left the door open between there and the kitchen so both rooms would warm up, and the small bedroom heater was sitting by the back door. I guess she hadn't wanted to wake me by bringing it in where I was sleeping. On the kitchen table was a note in Lester's bold scrawl: "Cass. Back for lunch. L." I read it, dropped it in the trash can, and got down the sack of Cat Chow.

"She must have been up for hours," I told the cats. "Didn't she sleep at all?"

They were too busy eating to answer, and I went out to feed Ronson. Sure enough, Lester's motorcycle was gone. I had no idea where she'd gotten off to, but I figured I had a fifty-fifty chance of finding out when she came home for lunch. It all depended on whether or not she thought it was any of my business.

I put water on for coffee and went out front to get the paper. Lisa was just getting out of her car in the drive.

"You cut a dashing figure in that getup," she called

as she came around the car, casting an appreciative eye at my pink flowered flannel.

"It's my new at-home look. What're you doing out at this hour?" I kissed her hello.

"Looking for breakfast."

"You've found it. Or the makings of it, anyway. My cook's gone off already, so we'll have to scramble some up for ourselves." The water was boiling merrily and I poured it into the top of my drip coffee pot

"I'm glad you've got heat at long last," Lisa said. "What happened? Weren't you as tough as you thought?"

"Lester got up before the crack of dawn and put the heaters in. Now she's off somewhere doing only-she-knows-what and says she'll be home for lunch."

I started to tell Lisa Lester's concerns about sex between butches, but something stopped me. I'd never talked to Lisa much about how I felt about sex; we'd always just done it, and what we both wanted seemed to agree. But I wondered now how my lesbian-feminist, college-educated, would-be social worker would react to what really worried somebody like Lester. There wasn't much sympathy these days for butch-fluff role-playing, even as styles of dress, much less in bed. Too patriarchal. I, though, could see where Lester was coming from, and although I like sex to be as completely mutual and reciprocal as it can be, I know that hesitation I sometimes feel about opening up, especially with a relative stranger, enough to receive as well as give in bed. I was lucky in my first lover, or I might have ended up like Lester myself.

Instead, I told Lisa about Lester's not planning to go to Sharla's funeral. "I couldn't figure out exactly why she didn't want to go, whether it was because a bunch of the rest of us were going or because of Sharla's parents, or what. Maybe she just hates funerals, or she doesn't want to deal with Sharla's death, or she's afraid she might cry and disgrace herself. Anyway, she didn't invite argument."

"So you didn't try to convince her to come?"

"Nope."

Lisa frowned. "Maybe you did right. You seem to know her pretty well."

"I don't really know her that well, but I know her type. She'd rather die than show weakness."

"Baby butches! I thought they were a thing of the past."

"You lesbian-feminists don't have the whole world sewed up yet, babe," I said, smiling. "There's still some of us real dykes coming along now and then."

Lisa rolled her eyes. "I don't know about you, Cass. You're as feminist as they come, but you won't call yourself one."

"Let's not go through *that* again." I handed her a cup of coffee. "Here. How about some scrambled eggs and grits?"

"For a change?"

"Just for the novelty of it."

We grinned at each other. It was a rare morning when I didn't fix scrambled eggs and grits for breakfast.

After we ate, I went to make the bed and Lisa went around to the other side to help. I saw her eyeing Lester's pillow, which still bore the imprint of her head. "I'm really grateful to you," I told her, "for setting me up with Lester. She's really something."

"What do you mean, 'really something?' "

I leered. "Oh, I just mean it's nice to have a warm body in the bed these cold nights, that's all."

"You have heat now."

"Not in here. We decided we didn't need to put this one in. I'm going to take it back out and put it in the rafters again."

Lisa threw a pillow at me, hard.

"Well, think of what we'll save on our gas bill, Lester and me."

She threw the other pillow.

"We just turn on our radio, nice and low, call KMFA and request Ravel's *Bolero*—"

"Cass, you're awful!" She looked around for something else to throw, wadded up the quilt and heaved it at my head. I fought my way out from under it and went on, "and then we get under this nice quilt like this...." I flung myself down on the bed, grabbing a pillow in my arms and pulling the quilt over me and it, writhing and twisting. "And then she does this, and I do this—"

Lisa leapt on top of me and wrestled the pillow out of my grasp. I grabbed her instead. The bed didn't get made up for quite a while.

I couldn't remember when I'd stayed in my pajamas until eleven o'clock in the morning when I wasn't either sick or hurt, but that's what happened this day. I hadn't gotten nearly enough sleep lately, and Lisa can always drop off any time, so after we made love for a while, we dozed a while more, and it was getting on toward noon before we finally dragged ourselves out of bed and got dressed.

"I feel more like breakfast than lunch," I said, and Lisa agreed.

"Do you suppose Lester would object to eggs and grits at noon?"

I laughed. "I'll bet it won't be what she has her mouth fixed for, anyway. How about pork chops and hominy, and maybe some nice green beans or something? I've got some nice pork chops."

Lisa agreed, and we worked on lunch together in a companionable, relaxed mood.

"Lester's late," Lisa remarked, glancing at the kitchen clock.

"She'll show up. She prides herself on her dependability. A rare and admirable trait in the young."

But Lester didn't show up. We waited until twelve-thirty and then ate, saving Lester some of everything, in the warm oven. When she wasn't there by nearly one, Lisa took the food out of the oven and put it in the refrigerator so it wouldn't dry out completely.

"Something must have held her up," Lisa said.

"Probably had more trouble with her motorcycle."

"She ought to phone, though."

"Yeah, but you know how it is. She's no doubt tied up somewhere and hasn't noticed the time. Maybe she's even at her parents'. They live here, and I bet she sees them a lot."

"Well, I'm not too sorry she wasn't here this morning, anyway." She smiled affectionately at me.

"I guess that wasn't too bad," I said, "considering you're a lesbian-feminist."

"And you're a pushover."

"What, me?"

"Yeah," she said, and kissed me. "You."

We could have gone on in this vein for a while, but I wanted to do a valve job on one of my lawnmower engines and Lisa had some people to see about carpooling to Sharla's funeral, so we separated for the afternoon. I went out to the garage and took the engine apart, and as usual when I get to working on something mechanical, I just lost myself in it and didn't even look at my watch for about three hours, during which time I de-carboned the head and cleaned and checked the carburetor, did the valve job, filed the points, and replaced a frayed starter rope. Then I remounted the engine on the mower, sharpened and balanced the blade, and tried it out on my back yard grass. It ran like a top and cut like a razor, and I was mighty satisfied with my afternoon's work.

I was just stopping the mower engine after finishing the back yard, when I heard the phone ringing. I ran to answer it, not knowing how long it had been ringing while the mower was making too much racket to hear it. I got to it in time, though, and it was a good thing, too, because it was one of my old and valued customers and she wanted me to come with her to pick up a whole bunch of shrubs she'd just bought on sale at a nursery. Her greed had gotten the better of her, she said, and she'd bought more bushes at those end-of-season bargain prices than she could carry in her car. So if I wanted to haul them for her and then put them in the ground next week, she'd be much obliged. I did indeed want to. I scribbled a hasty note for Lester and headed for the nursery to make a few bucks. It was a perfect October afternoon, bright blue sky and cool, light breeze, and as I helped the nursery employees load the shrubs in the back of my pickup, the sun was warm on my shoulders. I felt like singing, restrained myself for a bit, then decided, what the hell, and burst into a rousing chorus of *Heave Away, Santy-Anno* as I heaved the bushes up and into the truck. Mrs. Clark, my customer, smiled and beat time on the side of her purse as I sang. I do love October.

Chapter 11

I made it home before dark, singing all the way even though I noticed some clouds gathering in the northwest that looked a whole lot like rain. I hadn't heard we were in for a cold front, so I wondered what they could be. Things were a little on the dry side and we could use the moisture, but I was so enjoying the clear fall weather that I hated to see the end of it. Maybe these clouds were really nothing, or just a light shower that had come up for some reason.

I didn't see any sign of Lester's bike in the driveway, and the house was as silent as if Lester had never moved in. I went into the kitchen through the back door, expecting a note telling me she'd been and gone, but there was nothing at all. It looked like Lester hadn't been there, and that worried me a little. She'd been seeming so absolutely dependable that it made me wonder if anything could have happened to her.

"Don't be melodramatic," I told myself aloud. If Lester had gotten into some kind of trouble, at least she'd have called by now. Of course, I hadn't been here for her to call, and there was even all that time I was either out at the garage, though I was sure I'd have heard the phone from there, or mowing the back yard, where I knew I wouldn't have heard it. I'd feel awful if she'd tried to call and I hadn't answered. I hoped she hadn't needed me and found me absent.

I fed everybody and went out to the back yard with a beer to play ball with Ronson and wait for Lester. Ronson, tireless in retrieving, fetched the tennis ball to me over and over until my arm was ready to drop off from throwing it, and I finally had to call a halt. I wondered if he'd like to go hunting sometime. He wasn't trained to hunt, but it shouldn't take too much, I thought, to bring him up to snuff, his instincts were so strong. Of course, I'd only been hunting once in my life, and that was dove hunting where you really didn't need a dog. I'd fired the shotgun a vast number of times and hit a minute number of doves, of which I was just as glad when it came time to pluck and clean them. They were good eating, though, and the landscaping customer who had taken me out had given me a generous number of his, too. I'd fixed them with dumplings like you do chicken, and the woman I was with at the time and I had a feast. It made my mouth water to think of them now, the succulent, dark meat simmering in the pot with celery and spices and fluffy dumplings all floating on top. I went inside to check the refrigerator.

Lester's dinner was still there, untouched. I got out her food and started heating it up for my supper. When she came in, we'd have to scrape up something else for her to eat.

But Lester didn't come in. I finished eating and washed my dishes. I went to the front door to look at the sky and peer down the street, straining my ears for the sound of a motorcycle engine. I only heard the wind rising in the thinning leaves of the cottonwood next door and the faint roar of the Saturday night traffic picking up on Ben White, blocks away. The sky was rapidly clouding over from the northwest.

I went back in the house and turned on the radio, thinking to get a weather forecast. I got the World Series instead, and I wasn't really interested in it since the Astros weren't there. I turned the dial from station to station, but all I got were commercials and snatches of song or loud talk. I switched to FM and roamed up and down that band, too. Nothing I could relate to. I left it on KUT, which was having a program of old rock and roll that I remembered from my teenage years. I left it just loud enough to hear in the kitchen and went there to heat up some coffee.

Lester should really have called by now. Even if she'd tried earlier and hadn't been able to get me, she should have called back. I'd been home more than an hour. This, as far as I'd come to expect, wasn't like her. I poured a cup of coffee, ran some cold water in it at the sink, and sat down at the table to think about what I should do.

Maybe Lisa had heard something. I went into the hall and dialed her number. Elkhorn answered.

"Hey, babe," I said. I could hear the TV broadcast of the Series in the background, loud.

"Hi, Cass! Come on over and watch the game."

"I was looking for Lester, actually. Is she over there?"

"No, but Lisa is. You want to talk to her?"

"Yeah, please." The receiver clattered on a hard surface, and I heard Elkhorn's voice calling Lisa's name in the distance. A wild cheer went up from the crowd in Shea Stadium, cut off in mid-cry by an even louder beer commercial.

"Babe," I told Lisa when I got her, "Lester hasn't ever showed up and I'm getting worried about her."

"You don't have any idea at all where she might be?"

"None. She left before I got up, and I don't have the slightest inkling of where to start looking. But this just isn't like her at all—as far as I know. Of course, I don't really know her real well, I guess. . . ."

"But you're worried, anyway."

"Yeah. I don't know what I should do, if anything."

"I don't either. Who else does she know to hang around with?"

"I don't know. I can't think of anybody, really. She's not much of a socializer."

"No, she's not. Is there anything she needed to get done at her old place or anything? Maybe she went over there."

"No. Hell, I don't know. You know, I was just wondering . . ."

"Wondering what?"

"If it could have something to do with whatever it is she's been looking through all Sharla's old books and papers for." I told her about Lester's note taking and list making, and about how secretive she'd been being about it all. "So it makes me wonder if there's something she's investigating on her own about who Sharla was seeing and where she went that night that might have gotten her into some kind of trouble."

"Surely not. Nobody but Lester's ever hinted that Sharla had a date, or that the wreck was anything but an accident. Sharla was just out driving too fast or something."

"Yeah, but it does seem peculiar when you think about it."

"Oh, Cass, not you too! Leave well enough alone, won't you? The thing to do now is to think where Lester might be and call around and try to find her. Try some of Sharla's friends or something. Or call Lester's parents' house and ask them if she's there. You want me to come over?"

"Well...."

"I'm on my way. Don't worry, she'll probably be there by the time I get there."

"I hope so."

But Lester didn't beat Lisa home. I spent the thirty minutes or so that it took Lisa to get over to Hank Street from her apartment in one of those huge student warrens on Riverside Drive pacing around, racking my brain for clues as to where to start looking for Lester. I felt that calling her parents would be a waste of time. If she'd gone there at all, surely she wouldn't have spent the whole day. Unless there was some big, hairy scene and they'd kept her there against her will some way. Nah. They couldn't do that with Lester. Or could they? I'd heard horror stories about parents who had their daughters kidnapped by these cult-breaker types who held them prisoner and tried to rape, torture, and brainwash them out of being lesbians. If anybody did something like that to

Lester, I'd kill them. I went to look up Lester's parents in the phone book.

There were lots of Halls in Austin, I found out, and every one of them and his uncles and cousins and aunts, not to mention kids and grandkids, had telephones. I knew I'd heard Lester's dad's name at some point, but I was damned if I could think of it now. I was ready to howl with frustration when Lisa got there.

"Carvin," she said when I greeted her with the tale of my endeavor.

"Right! How could I forget that? It's like a big butcher shop: Carvin' Hall." I found the listing and dialed. No answer, not even after fifteen rings.

I hung up and dialed again, in case I'd dialed the wrong number the first time. Still no answer.

"Not at home, so I guess it'd be safe to assume she's not there, either."

"Okay." Lisa was making a list. "Here're the names and numbers of some of Sharla's friends, and most of them I know, so I'll do the calling."

I gratefully relinquished the telephone and went to make a new pot of coffee. It looked like it was going to be a long night.

Chapter 12

What Lisa turned up was interesting. Susan hadn't been home all day, so if Lester had come to see her, she hadn't connected. But Susan said that Marcy Johnson, whom she had run into at the market, had mentioned that Lester had arrived at her house at the crack of dawn, as she put it, asking if she knew anything about who Sharla had been seeing before she died. Marcy told her she thought Sharla had been completely wrapped up in Lester — though why, she'd confided to Susan, she couldn't imagine — and Lester had grunted and ridden away, "waking up the whole neighborhood."

I figured it had been at least seven-thirty and probably closer to eight when Lester had left my house, so I couldn't see what Marcy and her neighbors had to complain about. After all, it was Saturday, a working day for a lot of people. I grunted, too, when Lisa told me about it.

"So she couldn't imagine why Sharla was wrapped up in Lester, huh? And look at the types she goes with. You can't be around one of them for fifteen minutes without hearing all the same old, tired stuff you just heard from the last one you were around. And that must be the only little crowd left in Texas where everybody keeps saying, 'I hear you! I hear you!' every time anybody makes a statement. Always makes me feel like I'm talking too loud or something."

"They're just young, Cass. All that student crowd talks alike, you know that. It's just an attempt to fit in with their peers."

"Lester's young, too. But you don't hear her trying to imitate everybody she happens to be with. She's her own person."

Lisa laughed. "You can say that again. The only person I know who's more her own person is you."

"Well...."

"Anyway, I'm going to try Lucia. She'd be another logical one for Lester to get in touch with, and she wasn't at the bar last night, Kelly told me. We were trying to get in touch with her about going to the funeral earlier, but maybe she's in now." She checked her list and dialed while I hung around feeling useless and dashing to the window every time a car went by on the street. It was amazing how many cars sounded at first like Lester's motorcycle.

I was looking out the front door when Lisa walked up behind me and touched me on the shoulder. I jumped.

"Relax, it's me," she said. "You're pretty wound up over this, aren't you?"

I drew a deep breath and held it to get control of my nerves. "Yeah," I said when I'd let the breath go. "I guess I am. It's just so unlike her to go off and not come back when she says she will."

"Actually, we don't know that for a fact."

"Well, she's sure been dependable around me so far."

"Yes, but she may have just been on her best behavior, too. She admires you and wants to impress you, that's what I think."

A V-twin engine sounded in the distance, and I stuck my head out to look. Somebody on a Harley cruised by, trailing a cloud of blue exhaust smoke, which the eddying breeze swirled into the light from my front porch. I sighed.

"How can people keep running an engine like that? You'd think pride would make him fix it, if nothing else." I turned and paced back toward the kitchen, Lisa following. "I admire her, too. The way she's handling all of this shit about Sharla and all. I don't think I could do as well now, and I know damn well I couldn't have at her age."

"True." Lisa poured herself another cup of coffee. I hadn't drunk mine yet, so I picked it up and sipped. Cooled just right. I drank it down in a few gulps and poured another one. "She is holding together well," Lisa went on, "and I think she's leaning on you more than you realize. But, anyway, what I came out to tell you was that I still can't get Lucia. I get a real fast busy signal, so I called the operator and had her check it, and she said the phone's out of order."

"Damn. You think it'd be worth going over there?"

"Could be. But I want to call some more people first. If she's making the rounds, Lester'll have seen more than just Lucia."

So Lisa called Sharla's friends while I paced from the kitchen to the front door and back again several times, once or twice stepping outside to check the weather and look hopefully down the street. The sky was now completely overcast, and the wind had picked up enough to be feeling like rain was definitely on the way, and soon. And the report from Lisa, when she finished the last of her phone calls, was not much more than we'd known already.

She'd gotten Marcy Johnson, who just confirmed what Susan had told Lisa before, that Lester had been there before nine o'clock and had asked who Sharla'd been seeing besides her. Marcy had told the truth, that she didn't know Sharla had been seeing anybody but Lester. Lester had finally had to accept this answer and had left. "That motorcycle," Marcy had said, "gives us all a bad name. She's such a stereotype; I wish she'd grow up."

"There's never been a stereotype without some truth in it," I said when Lisa told me that. "I like a dyke who looks like a dyke. If we all looked like that, we'd be a lot better off."

"Or a lot better targets," Lisa said, "but don't get excited! Don't get excited! I like you the way you are, and I like Lester the way she is, so let's not get into that now."

"Well. . . ."

"I'm going to try Alleen next," she said, cutting me off, and started to dial the phone. I went back to look out the door.

Alleen wasn't home. Sandra Mary was, and Lester had been to see her about ten o'clock, asking the same question she'd asked Marcy. Sandra Mary had told her that Sharla kept to herself so much that there was no telling who she was seeing, if she was seeing anybody. Sandra Mary and Sharla had been lovers for a while and had parted not amicably, but had gotten back on fairly good terms lately. She was going to the funeral, and she and Lisa spent some time discussing transportation arrangements and funerals in general.

Laura Gant wasn't home, and she was a pretty close friend of Sharla's. Suzanne Alder was home but hadn't been all day. Her landlady who rented her a room had informed her that "a person" on a motorcycle had been asking for her, and Suzanne was not pleased with having to try and explain away Lester, who she'd recognized right away by her description—"a girl who looked just like a man, with white hair."

Obviously Lester was working hard at finding out what she wanted to know, but so far if she'd had any success, we hadn't found out about it. If anybody had known any secrets of Sharla's private life, it would have been Lucia, and her phone was still out of order.

"Let's try the bar," Lisa said after telling me her meager information. "Lucia might be there. Heck, Lester might even be there."

"She'd have called me, though."

Lisa patted my shoulder. "Lets go check it out," she said. We went in her car.

The bar was a relief after the quiet house. The music was deafening. The lights were dim and red, and the smell of beer and cigarette smoke were familiar and comforting. I looked around eagerly, but of course Lester wasn't there. Kelly and Elkhorn, regular Saturday night fixtures of the Hairpin Turn, were at home watching the game, and Tina was there but without Jacko.

"She's having dinner with her family tonight, so who knows when she'll be here," Tina explained.

I groaned. Jacko's family was definitely not good for her. By the time she got away from them, she'd be feeling guilty and resentful and depressed and angry and every other unhelpful emotional state I could think of, and she wouldn't be fun to be around at all. Tina knew it, too, and nodded agreement.

"Let me buy you a Shiner, Cass," she said. "We're all going to need something when she comes back from the semi-monthly ordeal."

"Okay, but in that case let me buy you another Lesbian Crush." I waved for the waiter.

"Fine." Tina grinned. "I'd love to have one on you."

"I think Cass has one on Lester," Lisa said. "She's fussing like a mother hen. Do you happen to know where Lester is tonight, Tina?"

But Tina, like everyone else, didn't know. I got my beer and circulated around among the tables, talking to women I knew. The only word I got was from Peggy Zorat, who said she'd been by Lucia's on the way to the bar to see if she wanted to come down, and Lucia had said she was having to stay home and work on a paper for her Victorian Lit class. I took this tidbit and hustled off to find Lisa, who I discovered dancing with a woman named Kathy that I barely knew.

I restrained myself with an effort and waited until the dance was over, then grabbed Lisa by the arm as she was heading for Kathy's table.

"I'm going over there," I told her. "I'll bet she knows something."

"How're you going to get there?"

"Damn!" I'd forgotten that I didn't have my truck tonight. "Can you take me home to get my truck?" I could see that Lisa was tired of looking for Lester and wanted to get away for a while, and if I had any more running around to do, I'd better have my own transportation.

"Sure," she said with a smile, quieting with a word the slight unease I felt on seeing her with Kathy. But then she undid that good work by saying, "Kath, I've got to take Cass home, but I'll be back."

"Okay," Kathy said. "I'll be waiting." And she touched Lisa's shoulder in an almost possessively affectionate way.

Well, Lisa and I were supposed to have an open relationship, anyway. It was just that we hadn't tested it yet. I wondered if she was using this little flirtation with Kathy to tell me how she felt about what she thought was my over-concern with Lester. I'd talk to her about it soon, I decided, but not tonight.

The ride back to Hank Street was pleasant, in the end. Lisa reached over and ruffled my hair when we got in the car, then sat a minute, looking at me, an amused expression on her face.

"What are you grinning about?" I asked her.

"You." She started the car and pulled out.

"What about me?"

"Just the way you are. I was feeling a little twinge of jealousy there for a few minutes tonight."

"What? About Lester?"

"Yes. But then I thought, what the heck, you'd get just as upset if I were out of pocket, so I quit worrying."

"That's right. I sure would."

"But you do have a little crush on her, don't you?"

"Oh, come on!"

"You think she's cute, don't you? Yes, you do, so admit it."

"Well, I guess I kind of empathize with her. . . ."

Lisa kissed her fingertips and reached over and touched them to my cheek. "Just don't break her heart, babe."

"Hell, I couldn't. . . ."

"And don't break yours, either." Her expression turned serious. "I don't want to see you hurt."

"Me? You don't have to worry about me."

"Well, sometimes I do, anyway. Do you mind?"

"No." I smiled at her. She was so beautiful; her face showing in profile against the light from the street lights as she drove was the loveliest I'd ever seen. It still surprised me a little that she could really care about me, we were so different in so many ways. It didn't surprise me that I cared about her, though, she was so handsome and so good-hearted and all the other wonderful things I could think of.

"Good," she said. "Then I won't tease you any more about Lester." She paused. "I do just want to know one thing, though, seriously."

"Okay."

"Have you decided who's the butch yet?"

I hit her on the arm. When we pulled up in front of my house we were laughing, and I wanted very much just to take Lisa inside and make love with her and forget everything else in the world. I saw immediately, though, that would have to wait. Lester's motorcycle was parked against the front porch.

Chapter 13

Lester was sitting at the kitchen table, polishing off a Whataburger and an order of onion rings. She had a milkshake, too. The radio was blaring from the bedroom, some awful rock and roll of the sort which doesn't seem to me to have any redeeming social value at all, and I was never so glad to hear it.

"Welcome home," I said, getting myself and Lisa a beer out of the icebox. "I was about to send out the National Guard."

Lester looked puzzled. "What do you mean? I'm not any later than I said I would be."

"The hell you say! This ain't lunch time, baby."

"Lunch time . . . ? Oh, fuck. You mean she didn't tell you?"

"Who? Tell me what?"

"Lucia. Goddamn bitch! I *knew* she was up to something. I'm gonna beat the shit out of her."

"Tell me *what?*"

"Where I was going, goddammit."

"Well, you're here now, so fill us in," Lisa said, pulling out a chair and sitting down.

"Yeah," I said. "Spill it. So Lucia was supposed to give me a message, huh?"

"Damn right, she was! That asshole. She said she'd call you."

"Why didn't you call me?"

"Because that bitch wouldn't let me inside her precious apartment, that's why! Goddammit, I'm gonna kill her. No shit. I'm going to. Jesus!"

Lisa leaned across the table and caught Lester's hands, which were knotted into fists, and said, "Easy, babe. Now just calm down and tell us from the beginning."

"There's nothing to tell." Lester looked down at the table top and didn't try to get her hands out of Lisa's grasp. I could actually see her shoulders relaxing. Lisa had that kind of effect on people. She'd make a hell of a social worker, if she ever left the plastics plant.

"So you went to ask Lucia if she knew who Sharla had been seeing, didn't you?" Lisa's voice was calm and low.

"Yeah." Lester looked up into Lisa's eyes. I might as well not have been in the room. "I just wanted to know, that's all. Because I *know* she was seeing somebody. Nobody believes me, but I know it! But nobody's saying anything. So Lucia, that damn bitch, she comes to the door and I ask her, as nice as pie, I ask her, 'Do you know who Sharla'd been seeing besides me lately?' and she goes, 'Oh, Lester, grow up,' with this little sweety-sweet smile. And I want to hit her, but I don't. So I say, 'Lucia, you were her best friend. Won't you please help me? I just want to find out why she ran off that road. If she was upset or something. That's all.' And she goes, 'Well, Lester, I might know who she was meeting that night, but I don't see how it concerns you.' Sharla goes running around on me and gets killed, and she doesn't see how it concerns me? So anyway, she finally says Sharla had a thing for this woman in one of her classes — which was just what I thought, from the way she was always going over to the library to study, she *said*, and I know there was this one straight woman she kept talking about, but I didn't think she'd be messing around with a *straight* woman." She waited for Lisa to reassure her at this point, and Lisa did.

"Maybe she wasn't really messing around. They were probably just friends. You know how that goes."

"No, I don't. I don't like straight women."

"Well, I don't think Sharla thought much about it one way or the other. We're all women, after all."

"Huh."

"But go on. Did Lucia tell you who she thought it was?"

"Yeah. Some het from Llano, she said. Or she said she thought she was from Llano. Some place like that, anyway. She's supposed to live on some ranch up there, and so finally Lucia said she thought the name of the ranch was the Box Bar, and I said I was going up there and hunt her up, and I asked could I come in and use her phone to call and tell Cass, and that bitch said no. She said, 'I really would rather you didn't come in, Lester, if you don't mind.' And I said I damn well did mind, and I had to tell you where I'd be, and she went, 'I'll call Cass and tell her what you're doing, but why she'd care, I don't know.'" Lester looked at me, and I rolled my eyes. She was right. Lucia really was a bitch. "So I told her to tell you I'd be back tonight, and if I wasn't back by ten, I'd call. And she said she would, goddammit!"

"Well, she didn't," I said, "and I'd about decided you'd been kidnapped or something."

"Her phone's out of order," Lisa said. "Remember?"

"Yeah, but that's no damn excuse, if she promised Lester she'd let me know. Anyway, all we know is, you can't call in. That doesn't mean she can't call out." I drank down the rest of my beer and got up to get another one. Lisa had drunk about a third of hers.

"I'm gonna kill that bitch," Lester said.

"But what happened in Llano?" Lisa said. "Did you find whoever it was?"

"Ellen Rowderburr. Sharla used to talk about her from her class. 'Ellen Rowderburr said so-and-so, Ellen said such-and-such.' I oughta have known. But goddammit, she was a straight woman!"

"Did you find her?" Lisa was patient as ever.

"Hell, no! I rode all the way up there, seventy or eighty miles, I bet, and looked in the phone book, and no Rowderburr. So I went to two different feedstores —"

"Good thinking!" I said.

Lester looked pleased. "And nobody had heard of the Box Bar Ranch or anybody named anything like Rowderburr. So I said, fuck it, and came home."

"Hell. So what do you think? Could Lucia have got it wrong about the name of the ranch or its being up at Llano?"

"The hell if I know. That's what she told me, though, and she sounded like she knew. And I know Ellen Rowderburr's the right name, because I heard Sharla say it enough."

"You didn't find an address or number for her in any of Sharla's papers?" I knew now what Lester'd been looking for in all that stuff.

"No. I think she just met her on campus. If she's from out of town, that'd make sense."

"Well, I wonder if Lucia could rethink things and come up with a better lead? If, say, I went over and talked to her sweetly."

"Now, Cass—" Lisa obviously suspected me of ill will toward Lucia for some strange reason.

"Well, why not? It was probably an honest mistake, and anyway, somebody ought to let her know her phone's out of order," I said through clenched teeth. "Right?"

"I'm gonna put her out of order," Lester said, wadding up her hamburger wrappings and slam-dunking them in the trash can.

"Now, both of you, just calm down." Lisa stood up, leaving her beer half-full on the table. "I'm going to run back to the bar for a while, so I'll just go by Lucia's and talk to her. You're right about telling her about the phone, Cass, and at the same time I'll see what I can find out. If there's anything new, I'll call you from the bar. Okay?"

What can you say to argue with the voice of sweet reason, especially when it's coming from somebody like my wonderful Lisa? I said, "Okay." Lester did too.

It wasn't until after she was out the door and off down the street that it occurred to me to question the fact that

Lisa was going back to the bar without offering to take us along at all. "I'll be waiting," Kathy had said. But surely there was nothing to it. Surely.

"Lisa's all right, isn't she?" Lester said, coming up behind me.

"Yeah. She's all right."

The first drops of rain slanted against the porch roof. I closed the front door and went to find my unfinished beer.

Chapter 14

"Cass, why don't you have a TV?" Lester was pacing around the living room, examining my rock collection on the coffee table, glancing at the books on the shelves, and now and then drawing the curtain back to check the rain pouring against the north window. I was sitting in the corner of the couch, trying to read a mystery and cocking an ear for the telephone bell. Lisa'd been gone for over an hour and hadn't called.

"I don't know. Just never got around to buying one."

"Don't you want one?"

"Nope. I see it when I go to people's houses, and I never see anything much worth watching. Except baseball, and I like that better on radio, anyway."

"How come?"

"Well, I can see it in my mind, you know. I bet the plays in my mind look twice as good as the ones on TV. And all those replays get on my nerves. If they call a guy out and I think he's safe, I don't want six different slow-motion views of his foot hitting the base after the catch is made to show me how wrong I was. I bet the umpires hate 'em."

We lapsed into silence. I realized after a while that I'd turned about the last three pages of my book without knowing a single thing I'd read on them. Lester was standing staring out the window by the front door at the rain falling through the light from the porch light. My watch read eleven-thirty, and Lisa hadn't called.

"I'm going to bed," I said. I got up and walked into the bathroom. I took a hot shower, trying to let my tension wash away with the steaming water, but it wasn't much good. She hadn't said she'd call for sure, just if she found out anything new from Lucia. Obviously she hadn't, so why should she go through all the hassle of waiting for the phone at the bar, which was always in use, and then spending a quarter just to tell me that? She probably thought I'd have been in bed an hour ago. With Lester.

Was that it? Was she carrying on with Kathy because she thought I had something going with Lester, for god's sake? Surely she couldn't think anybody could take her place with me. Hell, I'd let her know how I felt about her, hadn't I? Sure, I hadn't asked her to live with me, but she knew how I liked my privacy, and my house was really way too small to share. Of course, she'd stayed a while last year when I'd had my ribs banged up, but that was as much nursing duty as anything. She hadn't asked to stay, when I'd gotten back to work in a week or so.

I hadn't wanted her to stay, either. I'd needed to be alone, because I had some healing to do that was more than physical. That was after I'd gotten some emotional shocks from tracking down my long-lost first lover, and I had all that to sort out and come to terms with before I could get on with my life. I was just about all over that, but it'd taken better than a year. Maybe Lisa had just stuck with me until she thought I could take care of myself, and now she was ready to move on. And Kathy seemed like a nice enough sort, and she was good-looking, too. And a feminist. Don't forget that, I reminded myself. Lisa'd really be a lot happier with me if I could call myself a lesbian-feminist instead of just a dyke. I turned off the shower and started rubbing down with a towel. I probably hadn't left Lester much hot water. I'd stood there under the shower getting depressed for quite a while.

I walked naked into the bedroom the way I always did before Lester came to stay, and she was sitting on the edge of the bed with her pajamas beside her, waiting for me to get out of the shower. She looked startled when she saw me, and I was a little startled, too. I'd been so involved in gloomy thoughts I'd forgotten she might be there.

"Thought you'd died in there," was all she said. She vanished into the bathroom, and I put on pajamas and crawled into bed. The sheets felt smooth and the pillow was cool to my cheek, and I burrowed down and shut my eyes against the light and my mind against everything but the sound of the rain and the wind outside. I've learned to do that pretty well. I hardly knew when Lester turned off the light and slipped into bed.

Some time later, though — I don't know how much later because I'd been dozing — Lester said softly, "Cass? Are you awake?"

"Yeah."

"You sure?"

I grinned to myself. "Yeah, I'm about as sure as I can be. Why?"

"You were snoring."

"Well, I'm sorry. Next time just push on me or roll me over or something and I'll probably stop."

"It doesn't bother me. I just meant, were you sure you were awake, since you were snoring."

I rolled onto my side to face her and propped myself on an elbow. "I'm awake, anyway, so what do you need?"

"Nothing."

"Lester—"

"Don't get all hot and bothered, goddammit. I just meant it's not important. Go back to sleep, why don't you?"

"Okay, babe. It's important enough to wake me up, so what is it?"

"Well . . ."

"Come on. Out with it."

"It's embarrassing."

I tapped her shoulder a couple of times with my knuckles. "Now, here we are, two grown butches in bed together, you're even wearing my pajamas, and you're embarrassed to talk to me. And it's even dark, so you won't have to look at me while you talk, even." I paused, but she said nothing. "So out with it. It can't be all that bad. Nothing shocks old Cass Milam any more."

"I . . . well, it was what we were talking about last night."

"What?" It had been a long time since last night, as far as I was concerned. We'd been talking about Sharla, I remembered . . . oh, yeah, and about stone butches in bed, too. I'd bet that was it.

"You know . . .," Lester prompted.

"Oh, about letting a woman make love to you?"

Lester sighed. "Yeah."

"What about it?"

"Well, I've been thinking about it." She paused, and I stayed quiet and let her struggle with it. "I just . . . I can't imagine how you could let somebody *do* that."

"Well, you don't mind doing it to her."

"That's different."

I waited.

"Goddammit, Cass, I'm not a *girl*! I mean I am a woman, I mean, but I'm not . . . not like that. I mean, I'm *different*. You know? I mean, you aren't like that, either. You're . . . you're just . . . different. Not . . . I mean, you're strong and everything. You know?" The pleading in her voice touched me unexpectedly deeply. I did know. Boy, how I knew. It was the big reason I wasn't a lesbian-feminist, why I did the kind of work I did, why I dressed the way I dressed and cut my hair the way I cut it and walked the way I walked and thought the way I thought, and why I wasn't much interested in even being friends with women who weren't lesbians like me. I was different, and from the time I could first remember, I hadn't felt like I had much in common with girls. Boys, either, though. I didn't have any confusion about my gender. But I was definitely not like all the others, and I'd always known it.

"I know what you mean," I said. "You're right. You and I are different."

"So how can you let a woman . . . make love to you?"

"I told you last night. It's nice. Real nice. You just have to relax a little and let somebody else do the touching for a while, that's all."

She thought this over. "But, goddammit, *how*? How can you just . . . just let somebody make you . . . make your body . . . I just . . . Isn't that what you'd feel like with a man?"

I laughed. "I don't think so, at all. 'Course I don't know. I've never tried it with a man. But I think I could just about guarantee that's not what it's like."

"But doesn't a man . . . hell! This is hard to talk about."

"Yeah, it's not all that easy for me, either. But after all, if we can't talk about it, who can? I think it's hard for me to talk about because most dykes run like hell if you try to explain that you don't identify with the way all women feel. They think you're some kind of pervert."

"Sharla sure did."

"You and Sharla talked about this?"

"Yeah, some. But she thought she was just like straight women every way except she happened to like to make love with women instead of men. But she said it was just a choice she made."

"Yeah, that's what a lot of them say."

"But I know it wasn't a choice for me. I was just always a dyke. I always loved women. I didn't *choose* it! It's just how I am!"

I grinned at her in the dark. "Lester," I said, "I could kiss you. You can't imagine how nice it is to hear somebody else say that after all these years of hearing how woman-identified we're all supposed to be."

"Yeah, no shit. I thought I was the only one, until I met you."

"Well, you aren't. And nobody can tell me we're unique, either. I think this lesbian-feminist stuff doesn't account for a lot of what lesbians feel, but most dykes have bought the whole line and just closed their minds to what they really, deep-down know."

"Like Lisa? She's a lesbian-feminist, you said, but she's sure nice, and she looks like a dyke, too."

"Yeah, she's one, but I notice she's working in a plastics plant when she's got a perfectly socially acceptable job she qualifies for that would put her right in line with all that service to mankind stuff if she ever went to work doing it. So I don't know. It's beyond me, and I've about quit worrying about it."

Lester didn't say anything for a minute, and then she said, "But, Cass . . . if you let a woman make love to you, don't you lose . . . I mean, I get scared if I can't control what's going on."

"Oh, babe." I thought of when I'd first come out, and I'd had the same kind of thought, but it had only taken one try to make me realize that wasn't what happened at all. I tried to think of a way to explain it to Lester.

"Look," I said at last. "When you're growing up, you read all this garbage about how a man is supposed to be in charge of everything, especially in bed, and you hear about these rapes and you read these romantic stories about how the woman is supposed to be swept off her feet and surrender to the man, and I don't know if that's the way it is with hets or not. But it's just not that way with ordinary, down-to-earth dykes. Nobody's probably going to want to prove how they can dominate you or anything. You just want to give each other pleasure . . . only it's way more than that. It's . . . for me, good sex is like being connected to the power source of the universe; you just get all this tremendous energy, a lot more than the physical energy you're putting out. I mean, it's kind of like driving a race car, or flying a fighter plane. You're part of this huge, powerful, overwhelmingly exciting thing that's more than just you could ever be, and you just get into that and go with it, and it doesn't matter who's doing what to whom. Does that make sense?"

"Yeah. I feel like that sometimes. If I can make a woman feel really good, yeah."

"Yeah."

"But I . . . how could I give up control, though?"

"Well . . . you don't, really. Just like you don't really control the woman you're making love to."

"I do, too!"

"Maybe a little. But just think about it. Don't you pay attention to the way she's responding to what you're doing?"

"Yeah. Sure."

"And don't you try to read her responses and do what'll make her respond the best?"

"Uh-huh."

"So isn't she still guiding what's happening about as much as you are? It's a shared thing, babe."

"Well, maybe."

"Well, it is. Look, it's like flying a jet plane. You don't have to do all the controlling all the time. You can put it on autopilot and have that autopilot fly it for you. But you haven't given up control of the flight; you've just let an outside force do some of the work for you, that's all, so you can just lie back and enjoy the flying. But that autopilot won't do a thing you don't tell it to do, and if conditions change and you're not getting the flight you want, you can just give it some more instructions, or take back over yourself. See?"

"Makes sense. I guess. But it still scares me."

"Well, no law says you have to do anything you don't want to, so just take it as it comes and don't worry about it. And if you do decide to go that route, it doesn't mean you stop being who you are. Okay?"

"Okay . . . I guess."

The phone rang. Lester jumped like she'd been shot. I hopped out of bed and dashed into the hall to answer. It was Lisa.

"Cass?" Her voice was tentative.

"No, after midnight I turn into the Queen of Sheba."

"I forgot to call you."

"I noticed."

"I'm sorry, honey. I feel awful about it."

"It's okay. Did you find out anything from Lucia, then?" Honey? Since when was she calling me honey?

"Yes, I did. She deliberately lied to Lester about where Ellen Rowderburr lives."

"Well, I'll be damned. Why would she do that? And how the hell did you ever get her to admit it?"

"I got her drunk. Now don't say anything, because I'm not proud of it, but when I started talking to her I realized what she must have done, and it just burned me up. So I took her back to the bar with me and bought her three Lesbian Crushes and that was all it took."

"Well, I'll be damned."

"No, I may be. Anyway, Ellen lives on the Silverman Ranch out toward Johnson City. It's right on the highway on the right. You've probably seen it. It's that one with the miles of deer fence all along the road—"

"And the irrigated pastures down in the bottom of the valley? Yeah, I know it, all right. Wow! Does her family own it, or does she just live there, or what?"

"They own it, Lucia said. She said she didn't think people of that class would enjoy having their weekend interrupted by somebody like Lester—her words—on some silly wild goose chase, so she flat-out lied to her and sent her off to Llano. And she didn't call you because her phone was out of order and to go out and call would have been inconvenient, she said."

"Shit a brick."

"So that's the story, and I'm sorry it's so late."

"Yeah, it is a tad late, isn't it? It didn't take you this long to find that out, did it?"

"Well, no. But I just got to talking to Kathy afterwards, and the time just got away from me. You know how it goes."

"Oh, yeah. I know how it goes. So will you be over for breakfast to tell us all about it in great detail?"

"Uh, well . . ."

Sudden suspicion leapt into my mind. "Are you at home, Lisa?"

Silence.

"Or over at Kathy's?"

"Cass, I . . . yes, I am, but, ah, I'll talk to you in the morning, okay? Okay?"

I stared at the little bulletin board over the phone. There were still notes there from a couple of months ago. I was going to have to clear it off and get it in order. I don't like disorder very much.

"Cass? It's okay, I promise. I'll talk to you in the morning. I'll come over for breakfast. Okay?"

"Okay, babe," I said at last. "Good night." I hung up. I ought to get a better way to keep track of calls than that bulletin board. Maybe I ought to get an answering machine like everybody else had. I hate to talk to them, but what the hell, most people must not mind. I walked back over the cold floor to the bedroom and got in bed.

Lester looked at me, waiting for me to speak. I could see the shadows where her eyes were turned toward me in the dim light that filtered in from outside. I lay on my back and said nothing.

"She's at Kathy's, huh?" Lester said after a while.

"Uh-huh."

Silence lengthened. The rain was slowing down now, just a gentle fall that barely made a sound through the closed windows. In the dark, I lay and stared at the light fixture in the middle of the ceiling. Even with the light out, I thought I could faintly see there were dead moths collected in the bottom of it. I'd have to take it down and clean it tomorrow. I might give the whole place a good scrubbing while I was at it. A dirty house is depressing. The rain kept falling softly, softly outside, and the chill of October seeped under the covers and into my bones. I shivered, just a little.

Lester moved beside me, hesitated, turned on her side, took me in her arms, and kissed me as a lover.

Chapter 15

The rain had increased again by morning, and the house felt chilly and damp. I got up and lit the heaters in the living room and the bathroom, grateful to Lester for setting them up. Today we'd have to install the one in the bedroom, if the weather was going to stay like this. I went to get the paper from the front yard, dashing the few feet out and back and getting soaked in the process. I laid it in its plastic wrapper on the kitchen table, where it immediately began to form a puddle around itself, and went into the bathroom to dry off.

I put on water for coffee, unwrapped the paper and wiped off the table, sat down to read the news, gave it up, and got up again to pace to the front door and look out. It was about six-thirty, grey daylight. I went back to the kitchen and poured the boiling water in the top of the coffee pot.

This morning Lisa would be waking up at Kathy's. I'd never been to Kathy's house. I didn't even know what part of town she lived in, whether she had a house or an apartment, whether or not she had roommates — or even parents — living there. I hoped she lived alone, at least. I wondered who from the bar that I knew would be the first to start the talk around town about Lisa's new lover. I poured myself a cup of coffee and set it down to cool.

Grow up, Milam, I told myself. This is what an open relationship's all about, isn't it? Having the freedom to have sex with other people if the spirit moves you? You aren't married to Lisa, for god's sake.

A good thing, too. After last night, I couldn't talk, could I? I let my mind range back over what had happened after Lester had taken the monumental risk of kissing me. It had been obvious to me immediately that she was doing it largely because she wanted to comfort me about Lisa, and the risk she ran that I'd reject her, when I was one of the few people that had been willing to give her any support at all, showed a lot of courage. I could never resist a brave woman.

And so Lisa, my lovely and loving Lisa, probably had a new lover this morning, at least a casual one, and so, I guessed, did I. If I hadn't been so worried about what was happening with Lisa, I'd have been grinning from ear to ear this morning and whistling while I worked. Sex with someone new is exciting and fun for me, and especially if some neat, good things have gone on. And they had, last night with Lester. My young, butch buddy was a tiger in bed.

Even in the present circumstances I had to smile, thinking about the transformation that had occurred in Lester when she'd seen that I was going to accept her advances. There'd been no more of that tentativeness or uncertainty she'd shown earlier in our conversation. I could really see what she was talking about when she said she liked to be in control. She gave the word 'butch' a whole new dimension. And, at the same time, she was so tuned in to me and what I was feeling, it was almost like she was reading my mind. Add to that the fact that she really had her techniques down, and I stopped wondering how a snobby type like Sharla had lowered herself to be lovers with Lester. It wasn't something you'd be too anxious to give up.

I heard Lester get up and go into the bathroom, and I poured her a cup of coffee and set it on the table. She came in, in a minute, studying me sharply as she did.

"Good morning." I grinned at her. "I haven't figured out what you really like in your coffee, so I left it for you to fix."

"Morning." She looked at the black coffee, opened the refrigerator, took out the carton of milk, set it back without pouring any, closed the refrigerator, and sat down at the table. "You okay?" She frowned inquiringly.

"Yeah. How about you?"

"Sure." And then her frown began to give way, and she started to smile. "I guess I was ready for it," she said, "but, god, I still don't know what to think. I always thought you were just as butch as me."

"I know what I think. I think I didn't know as much as I thought I knew."

"Yeah?"

"Yeah. Have you ever thought about giving lessons?"

"Shit." She grinned.

"No shit. You could make a fortune, babe."

"Shit. What about you? You could talk the longjohns off a Methodist missionary."

"Maybe so, but I'd get bored with the missionary position."

"I didn't even know you knew the missionary position. You do that one, too?"

We both laughed. "Hell, babe," I said, "we hardly scratched the surface of what I do."

"Oh, yeah? You prepared to prove that?"

"I'll give it some consideration."

"You do that."

"I'll do that."

"I'm gonna hold you to it."

"I've been held worse."

So by the time Lisa, looking sleepless and guilty, arrived at the front door, Lester and I were relaxed and laughing over our coffee.

"Good morning, I see," Lisa said, taking in at a glance our silly grins. There was just a touch of ice in her tone. Here, she'd been feeling bad about being with Kathy and now she found me and Lester obviously sharing something nice, and it wouldn't take much to figure out what. She looked at me, naked under my terry cloth bathrobe, and at Lester in a flannel pajama top of mine and her jockey shorts and a pair of men's slippers.

"Yeah, good morning except for the weather, but it's okay for a Sunday," I said. "Sleep well?"

"I'm going for doughnuts," Lester said. "Y'all want any special kind?" She glanced nervously from Lisa to me.

Lisa smiled at her. "That's nice of you, Lester. I like those twisted ones, and those with the cream filling." She got out her billfold and handed Lester a five.

"Cass?"

"Any kind for me. And you better take my truck, hadn't you?"

"Take my car." Lisa tossed her the keys. "You'd have to move it to get out the truck, anyway."

Lester vanished into the bedroom, and we waited while she dressed quicker than a fireman and shot out the back door.

"Well." Lisa got herself a cup of coffee and sat down at the table with it. "I didn't sleep very well at all, as a matter of fact."

"You didn't?"

"No." She stared into her cup, then looked up directly into my eyes. "Cass, I'm feeling pretty mixed up about all this."

"All what?"

"You know all what. About Kathy. And about you. And about you and Lester."

"Okay, you're right, I know what you're talking about, and I don't mean to be nasty about it. I guess I'm a little uptight too, is all."

"She's nice, Cass."

"Kathy? Yeah, she seems to be. I don't know her, really. Where's she live?"

"Over in there behind the Unitarian Church, on Arroya Seca."

"She have a house?"

"Yes. She lives alone. Three cats and a chihuahua."

"Ah."

"The chihuahua's name is Alice."

"Nice name. You have a good time?"

"Yes." She sipped her too-hot coffee. I waited. "Did you?" she said after a while.

"Yeah."

"I thought so."

"Yeah. Well."

"Did Lester? Oh, hell, Cass, I don't have to ask that. Anybody can see she's crazy about you, anyway." She reached out to me across the table and we clasped hands, hard. "I am too, but I just—I just feel restless, or something. I don't know."

"What don't you know?"

"What I want, I guess. Maybe it's because I'm in this dead-end job at the plant, and I feel like I ought to be doing something in my field, I don't know. Anyway, it just all got to me last night, and Kathy was so nice and so uninvolved in all this stuff about Sharla, and she helped me get Lucia home after I got her confession out of her— I just went home with her, that's all."

"No, it's not all, babe." I gave her a smile.

"No, it's not all. And I didn't want it to be, either. But it doesn't mean I don't care about you . . ."

"I know. And my having sex with Lester doesn't mean I don't care about you, either."

"I think we're making this too big a deal."

"Maybe. Anyway, I think I'm too close to it all to see the forest for the trees right now, so let's leave it for a while, okay?" I squeezed her hand. "I love you, babe. That I do know."

Lisa squeezed back. "I know that, too."

I noticed she didn't say she knew she loved me.

We talked about different things that had gone on at the bar, speculated about how long Tina and Jacko were going to keep up their current relationship before they either split or moved in together, and read each other tidbits out of the morning paper. After a while, Lester came in with the box of doughnuts. She looked anxious at first, but when she saw things were peaceful, she settled down and joined in the conversation as much as she ever did. Lisa could always draw her out more than most people could, a skill that would do her proud if she ever did get into the social work she was trained for. After we'd about polished off the doughnuts, Lester took the help-wanted ads and went into the living room where she could spread the paper out on my desk. Lisa and I talked about this and that a while more, and I made another pot of coffee. The rain was still coming down steadily.

When the coffee was ready, I poured Lisa and me each a cup and took Lester's in to her. She was frowning with concentration and writing something on a notepad, but this time she didn't try to hide it from me, so I extended her the courtesy of not looking at it. I figured it was a list of job possibilities, anyway. It was, because she said, "I'm gonna find something this week or know the reason why."

"I'll bet you will. Here's some coffee." I put the cup down on the desk and dropped my hand onto her shoulder. She looked up at me then, and I read hope and anxiety in her expression, unmistakably mixed with affection. Damn. Lisa was probably right as usual and Lester did have a crush on me or something, and I was feeling so mixed up about Lisa and Kathy and all that, I didn't know how the hell I felt about anybody. I squeezed her shoulder and grinned at her. No matter what, I couldn't help liking Lester, rough-edged and unsocialized as she was. I hugged her head against my side, scrubbed my hand over her silky white hair, and kissed her quickly on top of the head. Then, I went back to Lisa in the kitchen.

"So, did Lucia give you any more dope on the mysterious woman from the ranch?" I asked her.

Lisa looked up from the comics. "Not really. Just what I told you last night. It's that pretty ranch up on 290 as you're going to Johnson City. The Silverman Ranch. Why? What were you planning to do, go up there?"

"You know me, don't you?" When Lisa and I had first met, she went with me part of the time while I was running around south Texas trying to find my first lover.

"Yes, I guess I ought to by now." She folded the paper and stacked it neatly in the middle of the table. "Just stay out of trouble this time."

"I'll take a first-aid kit."

"Well, I just have one thing to say about that, and you better remember it."

"What's that?"

"Discretion is the better part of valor."

"Oh, come on, babe."

She looked at me seriously. "I mean it, Cass. You never think you're going to get into any trouble, and then when trouble comes along, you jump right in with both feet."

"I do what I have to, that's all. Are you leaving us?" She was getting up and rinsing out her coffee cup.

"I need to get home," she said without looking at me. "I've got a bunch of stuff to do."

"Seeing Kathy today?"

"Yes. She's asked me over to lunch." She met my eyes defiantly.

I forced a smile. "Well, have a good time. Give her my better."

"Huh?"

"Give her my better. I can't quite say, 'Give her my best' just now."

"How about me?" she said after a second. "Do I still get your best? Or am I down to your better, too? Or maybe your good, or your bad? Or your worse? Or anyway, please not your worst! I've seen your worst, and I don't want it."

I thought of some of the times Lisa'd seen me at my worst. "No, definitely not my worst. I don't want to give you my worst. I don't know yet about the rest of it. Could be anything—except my indifferent. I'll never give you my indifferent." I looked at her, tried to smile, and felt like I didn't quite bring it off. I got a similar look back.

"Never is a long time, babe," she said.

"I couldn't ever live long enough to be indifferent to you, even if best comes to worst."

Lisa picked up her car keys from the table and walked to me, kissed me quickly, and started for the front door. "Goodbye, Lester," she said as she walked by.

"Bye," Lester said without looking up from her want-ads. I followed Lisa to the door, she opened it, glanced around at the rain still coming down, flashed me a quick little smile, and went out through the puddles to her car. I waited until I saw her get in and start backing out of the driveway, and then I closed the door. I didn't want to watch a ship out of sight right now. I suddenly felt kind of cold and shaky inside.

I realized I'd been standing there staring at the closed door when Lester came up behind me and said, "You okay?" with more concern in her voice than I'd ever heard there before. I mentally shook myself, then turned and took Lester in my arms. She held herself a little away from me so she could study my expression, and I managed a smile for her. Then she hugged me tightly, very tightly, and I clung to her like a scared kid to her mama.

"Lester," I said, "you want to go to bed?"

"No," she said. "I want to go to Johnson City."

Chapter 16

"How come you talk like you've been to college?" Lester, belted into the passenger seat of my Chevy pickup, turned at an angle toward me, one arm on the armrest and the other along the back of the seat. Somehow she managed always to seem poised for action.

"What do you mean?"

"You know. The words you use."

"Oh, like plant names? That's just part of my business."

"Yeah, I know that. But other stuff. Just when you're talking. You always sound like some kind of a schoolteacher or something."

I laughed. "I wouldn't last long as a schoolteacher with the language I use."

"You know what I mean." Lester was irritated. I was supposed to be answering her question, not kidding around.

"Yeah," I said, "I guess I do. It's just that I've always liked language, and I pick up a lot of it from reading."

"No wonder, with no TV."

"Anyway, I have been to college, babe. I took a couple of horticulture courses at San Marcos."

"Oh, yeah? But you didn't live down there, did you?"

"Hell, no. I was running a business up here with only me to do the work and running to the bar every night and courting a flock of women."

"I was gonna go to ACC, but I didn't."
"Why not?"
"Different stuff happened."
"You could still go, couldn't you?"
"I guess." She twisted in her seat to look out the side window, so I gathered the subject was closed.

We rode in silence for a while, me thinking only about driving on the slick road and about the fall landscape we were passing through, misty and dripping in the light rain, but beautiful with the seedheads of grasses and the yellows and browns of deciduous foliage not yet fallen from most of the trees. The highway rolled along through the limestone hill country, every now and then running along a high ridge where you could see across a valley to another line of hills, miles away. I thought of the ancient sea bed that made all this, all the creatures whose fossil remains washed to the surface of the grey-white road cuts. Every bivalve shell that had survived the eons since its maker died was now a little limestone heart you could pick up and weigh in your hand, heavier than life and a million times more enduring.

"You going tomorrow?" Lester said.
"I think so. I was hoping you'd ride with me."
"I don't know." She turned to face me again. "Cass, have you ever been to a funeral before?"
"Yeah. A couple. My grandparents'."
"Yeah?"
"Uh-huh."
"What're they like?"

I frowned, remembering. "Well, I guess there're different kinds. My grandfather's had a whole church full of flowers and a whole lot of people, and the preacher talked about the life he'd led and about all the good things people around the county remembered him for—he was district clerk in Angelina County for about thirty-something years—and it was kind of like a public tribute to him, I guess. I mean, I felt sorry, but proud, too. And then when my grandmother died, there weren't as many flowers in the church, and there were still a lot of people, but of course she'd outlived all her friends. She was ninety-four. And it was a whole lot sadder. I guess because I loved her more."

Lester didn't say anything. I remembered that beautiful, beautiful bright spring day, riding in the funeral home car to the cemetery, seeing all the flowers in the yards and along the roadside as we passed, thinking how Mama, as we all called her, would have loved to see it all. She'd worked in her yard every day of her adult life that weather would let her, until the arthritis in her knees had locked her in the house for good. She'd only seen spring through the window after that. I think I must get my gardening blood from her.

A deer fence arose beside the right shoulder of the highway, six feet high to keep the whitetails from getting over it. It dipped and climbed relative to the road level, following the ungraded contours of the rocky land. Then, through a gap in the roadside cedars, we could see an emerald-green valley of irrigated pasture grass far below the level of the road. There were ranch buildings in a clump with a little string of dirt road leading to them from someplace off to the west, and dark red cattle dotted the green near a pasture corner. The rain blurred the picture a little, so that it looked like a travel poster of the British Isles. It was the Silverman Ranch.

The entrance to the ranch was hard to spot from the highway, and I might have gone past it if I hadn't remembered where it was from driving this road before. I'd noticed it because it was strange to think of a ranch entrance you had to go through a cemetery to get to, but that's what you had to do. It was an old country graveyard, not the well-groomed kind you see in towns, with native grasses waving over the graves and the white limestone of the markers standing like outcroppings of the native rock itself. Here and there bright plastic flowers made dots of color among the grays and browns, and for once I enjoyed seeing them. They were cheerful on this rainy day. Lester's perpetual frown deepened as I turned the truck off the highway and steered my way along the rutted caliche road.

"What the fuck are you doing?" she finally asked.

"This is it. See?" I pointed ahead to a gate where a hand-painted sign announced that this was the entrance to the Silverman Ranch. "Bizarre, but true."

"Huh." Lester's jaw muscles worked. She fastened her gaze on the gate and looked neither to right nor left as we wound our way between the tombstones. It was not the happiest beginning our visit could have had, I thought.

There was a high gate with a sign saying to keep it closed. Lester opened it and reclosed it after I drove through, and then we were in the middle of fields so bright green they didn't look real. I drove slowly, taking time to look around at the well-built fences, the grass, and the cattle. Apparently the ranch took up the whole valley and I don't know how much of the surrounding hills, probably quite a bit. Too rich for my blood, I thought, and I said as much to Lester.

"Uh," she said. I thought I could see who was going to have to do the talking if we found Ellen Rowderburr.

I stopped in front of what looked like the main house and opened the truck door. "Coming?" I asked Lester. She opened her door without answering me and came splashing through the puddles around the truck, and we walked up on the porch of the ranch house together. Walking beside Lester always made me feel a little more self-confident than usual, just gave me that little extra assurance that comes with feeling like I'm not the only obvious dyke in the world. I felt like together Lester and I could lick anything. I grinned to myself, thinking that I hoped we didn't look too formidable to the person who opened the door.

I knocked, and in a minute the door opened. The woman who stood there was tall, about a head taller than me, and rangy-looking. She was dressed in blue jeans and a plaid shirt, cowboy boots, and a cap that said Co-Op Feeds on the front.

"Hello," I said. "We're looking for Ellen Rowderburr."

"I'm Ellen," she said, a question in the expression on her face.

"I'm Cass Milam and this is Lester Hall. We're friends of Sharla Doyle."

She hesitated, then said, "Come in."

Lester and I followed Ellen into the dry warmth of the ranch house, across a little hallway and into a big room with a fireplace. There was a mesquite-log fire, smelling sweet and homey as only mesquite can smell, and the room was lit with lamps, not overhead lights. It was a little too much on the dark side to suit me, looking a bit like something out of *Desert Hearts*. Ellen motioned us toward the couch in front of the fire, and she sat on a low stool with her back to the flames. I looked her over more closely. She was what I'd call fairly good-looking: regular features, clean, not unpleasant, but sort of bland for my taste. Her blondish hair was medium length, curling over her collar, and her long legs were bent grasshopper-style, the knees drawn up high and the slender arms wrapped around them as she perched on her stool. I could see Lester studying her, too. I wondered if Lester was thinking the same thing I was, that this woman didn't show enough marks of character to be a real dyke.

"You knew Sharla from school," I said, and Ellen nodded. "We were hoping to find out something more about Sharla's accident, and somebody said maybe you'd known where she was that night?"

"Oh, no." Ellen's voice was bright, too bright for the subject at hand, I thought.

"You didn't see her that evening at all?"

"Not that evening, no." She laughed nervously, her eyes flickering toward Lester and coming back to me. Lester saw the look.

"Look," Lester said. "You were seeing Sharla, and I know all about it. You know who I am, don't you?"

Ellen shook her head hard.

"I was Sharla's lover. Now, what I want to know is, I know she was sneaking around and seeing you, and I don't give a shit. But what I want to know is, what the fuck was she doing out on 2222 that night, and what upset her so much she ran off the road and killed herself? That's all I want to know."

"Oh, ah, Lester—" Ellen had to make an effort to get Lester's drag name out. "I, ah, I just don't know where Sharla was going." She bared her teeth in a completely insincere smile and spread her hands in a search-me gesture. "I'm sorry." Her tone was so bright and so condescending that even I wanted to pick her up and shake her, and I was afraid for a minute that Lester really might do it.

Instead, Lester leaned deliberately forward, pushing her face toward Ellen's and fixing her with a blazing glare. Her hands were braced on her knees and her back was stiff, and she looked like she was ready to launch herself at Ellen like an attacking pit-bull. Ellen tried to hold her ground but couldn't help drawing back, dropping her arms and shifting her legs to be ready to jump up and make a run for it. I thought about interfering, but I didn't, yet. Maybe I would, I decided, if it actually got physical.

"You're sorry?" Lester's voice came out low and menacing, about an octave below its usual pitch.

Ellen nodded rapidly, her hair bouncing above her shoulders.

"I'm sorry, too, Ellen. I'm sorry you aren't pleased to see me. I know *why* you aren't pleased to see me, and I'm sorry about that, too. I'm sorry you decided to take it into your head to mess with another woman's lover when you aren't even a dyke. I'm sorry you aren't a dyke, because you might not be such a shithead if you were. That's your hard luck, sweetie. But I want to know how my lover died, and I know you had something to do with it, or you know about it, and I plan to find out what you did to her if it's the last thing I do. Because that woman that's dead in a coffin up there in Dallas with all those shitass relatives around her and them denying everything good she was in her life, that woman was my lover, and I don't give a rat-fuck what anybody thinks, *I'm gonna find out what happened."* Her voice had slowly risen until she was almost shouting, but now it dropped again nearly to a whisper, and the whisper was chilling to hear. "And, Ellen Rowderburr, if you lie to me and I find out later you lied to me, I'm gonna be knocking on your door some dark night. And I don't think you'll be very glad to see me." She stopped speaking, paused for a moment, then slowly relaxed her rigid pose and eased back into a normal sitting position. "So, now." She smiled grimly. "What happened that night, Ellen? And how about the truth this time?"

Ellen, who'd slowly turned pale under the verbal assault, began to get some color back in her cheeks and tossed her head in a little, defiant gesture. "I already told you, I don't know what happened. I wasn't with her." But she sounded unsettled, and Lester went right after her.

"Forget what you told me. Maybe you weren't with her. Okay, I believe you."

Ellen started to smile, but Lester went on. "But I know you know what she was doing out there. Isn't that right? Because you did see her that night, didn't you?" Ellen opened her mouth, but Lester didn't let her get a denial out. "Oh, yes you did, so just tell me about it and I'll leave you alone."

"I don't know anything!"

"Okay. Say you don't. But I think you do. And you know what? I'll bet the cops'd like to know how that accident happened, too. So maybe I better just tip them off that you know something about it. That way you can come clean with them and they can tell the world, and I'll know what I want to know without you having to tell me, since you seem to find it so hard to talk to me without telling one baldfaced lie after another. How about that?"

Ellen opened her mouth, shut it, opened it again, and then dropped her face into her hands and sobbed. I didn't know what to do. I'm not at my best with straight women, because I don't feel free to touch them, but my impulse was to go to her and put my arms around her. I hate to see anybody cry.

Lester sat impassively watching. I looked at Lester and didn't even get her to glance my way. I looked at Ellen, shoulders heaving and cap knocked askew, and didn't know whether to feel sympathy for her or hostility, so I just sat there feeling helpless.

I didn't have to debate long, though, because Lester's shouting and Ellen's sobbing had been loud enough to be heard in another part of the house, and the sound of footsteps in the hall made me turn my head toward the doorway just as a very tall, black-haired man appeared there, saying, "Ellen? What's going—?" And then he stopped in mid-sentence, looking wildly from me to Lester, and leapt backward as if we'd shot at him. We heard him dash off down the hall, knocking over something with a crash as he went, and a screen door slammed in the distance toward the back of the house.

Lester said, "What the fuck?" and Ellen said, "Rod?", while I sat feeling more puzzled than startled. A car engine started behind the house, rose to a roar, and quickly dwindled in the distance.

"Who was that?" Lester demanded of Ellen, and Ellen, jarred out of her crying jag, said in a wondering tone, "My husband. But what in the world . . . ?"

"He going for the cops, or what?" said Lester. "Because that's just fine with me. You can tell them all about what you know about Sharla while I listen."

"He . . . the police? No . . . I don't . . . I can't imagine what got into him."

The guy, Rod Rowderburr, looked familiar to me, from the brief glimpse I got of him, but I was damned if I could remember where I might have known him. Maybe through one of my landscaping jobs, I thought. Anyway, he sure acted like he didn't want much to do with me and Lester.

"So, go on, Ellen," Lester was saying. "You're going to level with me now, aren't you? Tell me about what happened to Sharla that night."

Ellen sat silent, and Lester said, "Come on, Ellen. I'm not gonna hurt you. I just have to know."

"Ellen," I said, "if you're afraid somebody's going to find out about your relationship with Sharla and use it against you in some way, I understand, but I don't see what you think Lester and I can do with the information. We're lesbians, after all. We're not going to blackmail you or anything."

"No. Oh, hell." Ellen stood up and leaned on the mantel, staring into the fire. She took a long, shaky breath, then turned to face us. "Okay. Lester, you have a right to know, but I really don't know very much. It's true Sharla and I had been seeing each other a lot, and I guess maybe I led her on in a way. I'm in the middle of a nasty divorce, and she was so sympathetic and easy to talk to—I just got a crush on her, I suppose. And she got one on me, too. I guess you know all about it, or you wouldn't be here."

Lester nodded. "I knew it was somebody."

"But, believe me, nothing ever happened. Nothing, really. Oh, I . . . we just kissed a little. It was nothing, I swear, that's all there was. Really." She looked anxiously from one of us to the other.

"Yeah, sure," Lester said.

"Now, Lester . . ." I said.

"Well, nothing *really* happened . . . much." Ellen said, and Lester sighed.

"You mean you didn't get around to breaking the sodomy law?"

"Lester!" I said. The woman was admitting enough; I didn't think we needed all the gory details.

"So anyway," Lester said, her voice overriding mine, "you and Sharla were 'seeing each other,' as you might call it, and one of the times you saw each other was the night she died, wasn't it?"

"Yes, it was. But not for long. She met me at the library—she'd called me here that morning and asked if she could—and we just saw each other for a few minutes. And I really don't know what was on her mind, because she never really said. I thought she was going to tell me something or ask me something important, but she didn't. We just chatted for a few minutes about nothing, and she kissed me and left, and I never saw her again. The next thing I knew was when I read in the paper she'd been killed." Ellen's voice was under tight control, but I could hear the emotion under the surface.

Lester, however, had a different reaction from mine to what Ellen had said. "*Sharla* kissed you in the *library?*"

"Yes."

"My god." Lester looked stunned. "Were there *people* there?"

"Of course not! We were back in the stacks. Of course nobody could see us!"

"Shit."

I could see Lester was either sidetracked or completely derailed by this revelation about Sharla's public behavior, so I thought I'd better get the rest of the relevant information out of Ellen while the getting was good. "Did she say where she was going when she left you, Ellen?" I said.

"No. She said she had an appointment."

"No hint about who or where?"

"No."

"Well, do you remember what it was you did talk about, then?"

She shook her head. "Not really. I talked about the divorce some. About the ranch. I don't remember."

Lester stood up suddenly and said, "Let's go." She headed for the door.

I stood, too, and looked up at Ellen's tear-streaked face. We hadn't been fun guests this Sunday afternoon. The front door slammed, and Lester came into view through the front window, marching through the puddles toward the truck with her head down.

"Sharla didn't think Lester loved her, but I believe she did," Ellen said.

"She did," I said. Ellen offered her hand and I took it, held it for a minute, and then, because this wasn't just any straight woman, I hugged her. She hugged me back, and I followed Lester out into the rain.

Lester sat brooding as I started the truck, turned it around, and drove off along the road through the ranch. I thought back over the visit, a little fragment here and there, not able to get much out of it yet—except that I'd hugged Ellen, and remembered the novel sensation of having to reach up to get my arms around her. She was taller than me by a good bit, taller, maybe, than Elkhorn. She and her tall husband, Rod, made a good match for height, at least, though from what I'd seen of him, he was taller yet. I'd have to bend my head back to talk to him like Jacko had to me, like I'd had to recently—when? —to talk to somebody. . . .

"I'll be damned, Lester," I said. "Do you know where I've seen her husband before?"

"No."

"Think, Lester. You saw him, too. Don't you remember?"

"No. . . . Wait! Ape arms? The fag in the red shirt? The one Sharla was talking to?"

"Right. The one she was talking to in Houston. In the Orchid Room."

"And what do you bet," said Lester, "his dyke-loving wife doesn't know he's a fag?"

Chapter 17

Coming back from the ranch in the grey afternoon, Lester and I had talked over the visit only briefly and then lapsed into silence. Neither of us knew what to make of what we'd learned from Ellen or of what we surmised about Rod Rowderburr. It was obvious that Sharla must have had something on her mind when she made the date to meet Ellen that she'd decided not to bring up by the time they actually met, and it was plain, too, that she was going somewhere to see somebody afterwards, and that it was in coming back from that meeting that she'd run off 2222 and died. But we really didn't know much more than when we started, when all was said and done. The dark day and the rain wore on our spirits, and we sank into our separate quagmires of thought, two unhappy dykes that couldn't help ourselves or each other.

Lisa and Kathy kept appearing in my mind like Banquo's ghost, spoiling for me what at other times would have been a feast of autumn scenery and hill country views. I usually like rainy days, but this wasn't shaping up into one of my favorite Octobers. Well, it would be over by the end of the week. Halloween was Friday. Anybody, I figured, had a right to be depressed in November, and I planned to exercise that right beginning Saturday. Meanwhile, I had an exhausting drive to and from Dallas to look forward to tomorrow, darkly highlighted by Sharla's funeral. I had to settle travel arrangements tonight about who was going in which vehicles, and I had to get a definite answer out of Lester about whether she was going at all or not. If she wasn't, I felt like I ought not to go, either. I really couldn't see leaving her alone in Austin while we buried her lover.

Across from me on the other side of the truck, Lester stared out the window at the passing scenery and brooded. She only spoke once as we were getting into the outskirts of Oak Hill, just about to the Austin city limits. "Is that a helianthus?" she said.

"What?" I was startled both by the suddenness of the speech and by its content.

"Cass, goddamn it! Do you *have* to say 'what' *every* time I ask you something?"

"Sorry. You startled me. I was thinking about something else. Was that a helianthus? Yeah, if you mean those tall stalks with the yellow flowers up and down them."

"Yeah."

"Yeah, that's *Helianthus maximiliani*. The Maximilian sunflower. How'd you know that?"

"You showed some to Lisa on the way to Houston."

"Yeah, I did." I'd have thought Lester would have had all her attention on fighting with Sharla during that ride that seemed like a year ago now. But she didn't miss much, as I was learning from being around her more. That was a quality I noticed in nearly all of the dykes I liked, especially the butcher and more obvious ones of us: an alertness to everything that went on around us. It was a good survival trait for us social pariahs to cultivate. It's not healthy to wander around in a little world of your own when you're fair game for every frat rat, drunk prick, and fundamentalist Christian in town. I've always thought that must have been what the Daughters of Bilitis founders were thinking of when they adopted "Qui Vive" as their motto.

I found it kind of touching that Lester would have been paying enough attention to me on that Houston trip to remember something like the Latin name of a flower that I'd mentioned. I'd been trying my best to ignore her and Sharla. But I'd still had Lisa then.

I still have Lisa now, I told myself. I have her just as much as I ever did. This is just part of having an open relationship, and I'm doing the same thing she is, just expressing my sexuality with a different partner, that's all. It doesn't mean we don't love each other. But it might mean, I argued back, that we'll never be lovers again. We might just be friends. Casual friends. Friends that don't see each other but once in a blue moon, when neither one has something else going. Friends that never take their clothes off and get into bed together and kiss and touch and look into each other's eyes and feel everything they know about themselves and each other, everything they've shared for so long, all the knowledge and skill they've gathered in loving each other and pleasing each other all come together in that incredible, overwhelming surge of power and joy that not all the Latin-based terms for it in the world can begin to describe. And never lie together again in the warm darkness, relaxed, at peace, happy, one's head on the other's shoulder, drifting, surrendering to sleep, secure in ourselves . . . safe for once, safe at last. . . .

I clenched my teeth and told myself to stop this kind of thinking. No matter what happened, and nothing really had yet, to part me and Lisa, at least she was still alive. Poor Lester's lover was dead. That kind of never is a really long time. Where there's life, there's hope, I told myself. But I still didn't feel too hopeful.

With these gloomy thoughts circling in my head like vultures, I pulled into my driveway on Hank Street. It was, as usual, good to get home.

Inside the house, Lester went to change out of her damp clothes while I lit the heaters. It was not really cold, but I wanted to drive off the dismal dampness. I lit the heaters in the living room and the bathroom, then found Lester had already taken care of the one we'd finally gotten installed in the bedroom. She was adjusting the flame when I walked in.

"Oh, good," I said. "You've got this one."

Lester straightened up and faced me, looking earnestly into my eyes. "*Now,*" she said, "I'd like to go to bed. If you still want to."

I threw my arms around her and hugged her as tight as I could. "Why not?" I said, and she hugged me like a bear.

I kissed her, standing there, and she kissed me back, the two of us kind of sparring to see who was going to get the advantage of the other, and then I told her, "Easy, easy," and backed off a little, and we slowed things down a bit, and I could feel her breathing start to deepen along with mine, the fight in her giving way to a softer sensuality that set me on fire. With Lisa it had been her grace, her suppleness, the smoothness of her skin that had done this to me; with Lester it was the solid feel of her body, her strength, and her willingness to gentle that strength for me that made me want to lose myself in her arms. We staggered like drunkards to the bed and sank down together. I rolled onto my back, carrying her locked against me, and I looked up into those deep blue eyes that had seen so much for one so young. "Oh, Lester," I said, and she smiled down at me, still watching me as she lowered her face to mine, and the phone rang.

Chapter 18

We stood in a puddle on the concrete front porch of Kathy's house on Arroya Seca, Lester having been persuaded with some difficulty not to wait for me in the truck, and I knocked on the screen door, there being no doorbell. Kathy, when she opened the door to us, looked different from the way she did at the bar. Under the red lights of the Hairpin Turn she looked younger and smoother than she did now in the daylight. I hoped Lisa had been shocked when she woke up this morning and saw her. But she probably hadn't. She'd always liked my thirty-nine-year-old looks, after all. I cast an eye at Lester, who was scowling ferociously, and winked. Lester pretended not to see.

"Come on in, you two," Kathy said. "Lisa's back in the kitchen controlling the watchdog." A sharp, rapid yapping had been going on ever since I'd knocked. Kathy led the way to the kitchen, and Lester rolled her eyes and gestured for me to go ahead. I did.

The kitchen was bigger than mine but not as clean, I noticed to my pleasure. There were dirty dishes in the sink, a couple of cups and glasses on the counter, and a pan on the stove with the remains of something in it. I looked around and smiled.

Lisa was sitting in a wooden chair at the formica-topped table at one end of the room holding a tan chihuahua in her lap. The little dog was yapping its head off, teeth bared and tiny body straining to escape from Lisa's grasp.

"Alice, these are friends," Kathy said in a squeaky voice. "Cass, Lester, this is Alice."

"Yap, yap, yap, yap," said Alice, slobbering at the little jaws.

Kathy swooped Alice out of Lisa's hands and cuddled the enraged animal to her skinny bosom. "Now, Alice, we must be nice to the nice people who've come to fix Lisa's car."

"Grrrrrr," said Alice.

"I don't know what's got into her," Kathy said, gazing at us soulfully over the three pounds of fury in her arms. "She usually only acts this way with men."

"Let's see your car, Lisa," Lester growled, provoking Alice to a renewed frenzy.

"It's in the drive at the back," Lisa said. She got up and led us out the back door. Kathy, as we left, was saying, "I'll just stay and calm Alice down, Leese. You know I'm no good with cars, anyway." Lester, bringing up the rear, closed the kitchen door so hard the glass in it rattled. In the room behind us, Alice went into paroxysms of yapping.

Lisa's Toyota, looking grey instead of silver in the dismal light, sat dripping and lifeless in the driveway as Lisa cranked the starter with the key.

"It's not gonna fire," Lester said. "Lisa, pull the hood latch." Lisa did, and Lester and I dived under the hood.

"Where *is* anything on this damn engine?" Lester said.

"Damned if I know. I've never looked at it before." We both started reaching around, pushing on electrical connections, wiggling wires, peering under and between the mess of hoses and belts, looking for anything that might be obviously wrong. After a while we had established that gas was getting to the carburetor and that there was apparently no spark.

"Damn pointless ignition," Lester said. "High-tech shit."

I shook my head at Lisa. "It's beyond me, babe. We're going to have to tow it, looks like, unless you can think of anybody else that might know more than we do."

"No. I can't think of a soul. And dammit, Cass, how am I going to get to Dallas tomorrow?"

"Ride with us, of course."

"I'm not going," Lester said.

"But I was taking Kathy . . ."

"Well," I said reluctantly, "we've ridden with three of us in the truck on a trip before . . ."

"Unless I can take my motorcycle in the back of the truck, so I'll have it to ride in Dallas," Lester said quickly. "I could use your tiller ramp to load it, couldn't I, Cass?"

"What?"

"To load it. My motorcycle. In your truck."

"Oh, uh . . ."

"Cass, Kathy doesn't have to go. She really doesn't much want to," Lisa said.

"Well . . ."

"Oh, sure, let her come," said Lester. "I can ride in the back with my bike. I just hope it's not raining too hard."

Lisa suddenly laughed aloud, grabbed Lester in a big hug, and kissed her. "You'll ride in the front with us, you idiot," she said. "I'll tell Kathy she doesn't have to go."

"Well," I said.

"Come on. Let me get my jacket and we'll go. I can deal with the car after we get back. I should have worn the jacket out here, anyway; I'm frozen stiff."

We trooped back into the house, and Lisa told Kathy, "No luck! Can I leave it here until Tuesday? I won't have time to get anybody out here tomorrow."

"Of course, Leese. I don't use the drive, anyway, for my bike."

Lester pricked up her ears. "You have a bike? What kind?"

"It's a Schwinn."

"Oh," Lester said. "A *bicycle*."

"So, Kath, can you get another ride to Dallas?" Lisa said. "I'm really sorry, but maybe Jacko could squeeze you in and I can go with Lester and Cass in the truck."

"Oh, I'll find something." Kathy flashed Lisa a brilliant smile. "I'll see you up there, probably."

"Fine." Lisa paused. "Well . . . I guess we'd better be going . . ." She looked at Kathy with distress. I knew damn well they wanted to kiss goodbye, and I bowed to the inevitable. I'd rather just know about it than actually watch it.

"Come on, Lester," I said. "Lisa, we'll be in the truck." I reached for the knob to open the door from the kitchen to the living room. Kathy noticed just too late and shouted, "Don't!" But the door was already opening when she said it.

"What—?" I began, and Tiny Alice shot through the doorway and sank her teeth into my ankle.

Chapter 19

Lester drove, pointedly giving driving all her attention. Lisa sat in the middle, eyes straight ahead. I sat by the passenger door, leaning into it, welcoming the cold touch of metal rather than the warmth of Lisa's body against mine. Nobody spoke.

Lester went down Guadalupe to MLK for some reason known only to her, and I stared contemptuously at the students and university hangers-on wandering along the Drag in front of the closed shops. College-educated and too stupid to come in out of the rain. Maybe you had to get a master's degree like Lisa's before you got any sense. Maybe even that didn't do any good. It was cold in the truck, but I wasn't about to lean across Lisa and turn on the heater. The windshield wipers squeaked like fingernails on a blackboard, over and over. My ankle hurt.

Lester turned left on Martin Luther King, which I still thought of as 19th Street, and headed for I-35. A sleek little green car with froggy eyes cut in front of us, and Lester braked expertly on the slippery pavement and said, "Cocksucker!" under her breath. Lisa made a sound between a sigh and a snort, blowing a short jet of air through her nostrils. Lester signalled and got in the right-hand lane.

I was surprised when she braked and turned right onto Brazos. It wasn't a good way to get anywhere that we'd want to go. But I wasn't driving, and I was damned if I was going to be the one to break the ice by speaking. It was probably too solid to break, anyway. The best I could probably do would be chip at it, and I wasn't up to it. Brazos ended at a State building in two blocks, and Lester made another right, and then a left on Congress. I've always liked the back-door approach to the capitol; it makes it seem more accessible to me than it looks when you come up Congress from the other way and see all that impersonal granite looming at the top of the hill. Lester went on into the capitol grounds, following the counter-clockwise drive under the dripping trees, and parked illegally in a legislator's slot. I glanced apprehensively around for the guard that would usually emerge from nowhere to run us off, but nobody much was around this late Sunday afternoon.

Lester took the keys out of the ignition and stuffed them in her pocket and opened the driver's side door.

Lisa broke down first. "Lester, what are you doing?" she said in a peeved tone.

"Going for a walk." She got out and closed the door. Lisa slid quickly over to that side, opened the door, and called, "Lester!" to her retreating back, but she just kept walking, across the drive, along the sidewalk, and out of sight around the front of the building.

"Well!" Lisa said.

I didn't say anything. Lisa sat behind the wheel and drummed her fingers on the top of the steering column.

"I'd let you take it for a spin," I said, "only I don't seem to have my keys."

Lisa stared at the windshield.

"It's a nice truck to drive."

No answer.

"Lester does it well."

"Yeah." Lisa turned to glare at me. "You probably ought to know."

"Oh, now, say —!"

" 'Now, say,' yourself! God, Cass! I've never been so embarrassed!"

"Well, now, wait a minute . . ."

"I will not wait a minute. There I was, sitting there all day telling Kathy how wonderful you were and how kind you were being to poor Lester when she needed a friend, and what a neat person you were, and then you act the way you did—I could have died!"

"Well, hell, the damn thing bit me, for Christ's sake! What did you want me to do, give it a medal?"

"You didn't have to kick her!"

"Kick her! I didn't kick her! I was just trying to shake the damn thing loose, that's all! It had its *teeth* in my *ankle*, Lisa. And in case you can't imagine that it hurt, just take a look at it!" I jerked my leg out from under the dash and yanked up my pants leg. The bite wound had bled, leaving a crusty, dark streak down the white skin and a stain on the ribbed cuff of the sock. The flesh all around it was swollen and already turning ugly with bruises. Lisa glanced at it and looked away.

"I don't care," she said. "You could have let Kathy take her off and it wouldn't have torn your ankle up."

"Yeah? Well, when, I wonder, was Kathy planning to take her off? Because all I saw Kathy doing was yelling, 'Alice, no-no,' and laughing."

"She wasn't laughing, Cass."

"Well, she was sure as hell about to bust a gut trying not to, then. She thought it was damned funny, and you know it."

"She didn't think it was funny when Lester nearly broke Alice's jaw."

"Lester was the only one there trying to keep the damned little shit from chewing my foot off. All *you* were interested in was criticizing my choice of words."

"And that's another thing! How *could* you use that term? You're a lesbian, Cass, even if you aren't a feminist. I'd think you'd at least avoid heterosexist terms of derogation."

"Oh, boy. Pardon me, I mean, 'oh, person.'"

"Cass, really . . . !"

"Yes, really! You keep telling me I'm a feminist whether I think so or not, and now you tell me I'm not one, just because of a word I happen to use. And that word, in that context, might not have been exactly feminist, but it sure ought to qualify as *lesbian*-feminist."

"It's an anti-gay-male term!"

"No, it's not. If I called a male dog a cocksucker, that would be anti-gay-male. But I didn't, did I? No, I didn't. In fact, what I said, and I remember exactly, was 'cocksucking bitch.' Which indicates *hetero*sexual conduct. Doesn't it? And I'd think I, as a lesbian, as you so cleverly point out I am, ought to have a perfect right to make derogatory statements about heterosexual conduct and the bitches who practice it."

"NO YOU DON'T!" She sucked in a breath and lowered her voice. "No, you don't, Cass. Because we're women first, and then lesbians. Being a woman is part of the definition of lesbian. And for us to criticize other women's conduct, just because it's different from ours, just isn't right. It doesn't even make sense. God, you ought to know, with the work you do, how people look at women in this world. I just really can't believe you don't understand that. I don't see how you can expect them to respect your sexual choices if you refuse to respect theirs. I just can't."

I've never been good at arguing religion or politics. I couldn't even tell which of those this was. I just knew it wasn't something Lisa'd thought up by herself. I didn't say anything.

It was really getting chilly in the truck. Lisa was hunched up in her jacket, watching the misty rain gather into drops and snake suddenly down the windshield. My ankle was throbbing down there in the cold. It was getting dark. Lester finally appeared in the dusk and opened the truck door. Lisa slid silently over to let her in.

"Y'all get it worked out?" Lester said.

Lisa shook her head, not looking at either of us.

"Yeah," I said.

"I've got to get home," Lisa said.

"Okay." Lester started the truck. "You sure?"

Lisa nodded. Lester shrugged and backed out of the parking space. We rode the rest of the way to Lisa's apartment in silence.

Lester drove around the labyrinthine parking lots that surrounded the buildings where Lisa lived and found a parking place under the death-pale glow of a mercury vapor lamp. I got out, being careful not to put too much weight on my hurt ankle, and stood aside for Lisa. In the light of the mercury lamp her skin looked bluish silver, unreal. The whole situation seemed unreal to me. How could this be happening? I felt an anguish I hadn't known in years. Lisa, unless I could say something or do something to prevent it, was going to leave me.

Lisa started walking toward the iron stairway that led up to the second floor of the building and the door to her apartment. But she wasn't stalking off like she was mad; she was moving slowly, reluctantly, head down in the misting rain. I moved to get back in the truck, then checked myself, closed the truck door, and followed her.

She didn't stop when she heard me coming, but she didn't speed up, either. I caught up with her in a few strides, ignoring the hurt in my ankle. We walked together to the foot of the steps.

Lisa stopped there and turned to me. "You better not try these stairs with that ankle," she said.

"It's okay."

She stood hunched in her jacket, the collar turned up around her face, her hands in her pockets. She looked colder than the rainy night. I wanted to hold her, to warm her and protect her from hurting. I half-reached out to her, then dropped my arms to my sides. We stood there for a minute, neither of us speaking.

A little, cold wind swirled the mist around us. A flurry of bigger raindrops swept across the parking lot and subsided to mist again. Still we stood there, hopeless, but holding on. I felt a hollow place inside me. I thought she surely must feel one inside her, too.

A car pulled into the lot and parked, the driver gunning the barely-muffled engine before turning off the ignition. Four people, two het couples, got out and dashed, laughing and shrieking, toward another stairway and thundered up it to the second floor, the iron clanging under their pounding feet. Loud, male laughter split the night; two or three of the bunch talked at once, and then a door slammed, cutting off the sound.

"Lisa," I said, "I'm sorry."

"It's okay, Cass." Her voice was bleak.

"I'll try harder. I really will, babe."

"I really like Kathy." She looked at me in distress.

"I can see you do."

"It doesn't mean I don't like you, too."

"But it means you . . . don't love me, though."

"No. It just means . . . it doesn't mean that."

"Do you want me not to sleep with Lester?"

She sighed. "No, that really doesn't bother me. Oh, I wonder what you do, I guess, and I worry a little that maybe she's more what you want than I am. But it's your business, and I know you'll be honest with me about it."

"Yeah. You know I will. But, oh, babe, she's not you. She couldn't touch you!"

"But she loves you."

"No, she doesn't. Or, hell, I don't know, maybe she does, in a way, for right now. Maybe I feel the same about her, but it's not like with you, Lisa."

She put her arms around me then, and we held each other as hard as we could. Finally we drew apart, and Lisa said, "Babe, I'm just all mixed up. Can you give me some time?"

"Yeah. I can give you that."

"I do love you, Cass."

"I love you, too. Lisa, I really do."

"Will you still take me to Dallas, or would you rather I rode with Kelley and Elkhorn?"

"Which would you rather?"

"I don't know." I waited, watching her think about it. Finally she said, "Maybe it'd be better if I went with them."

"I guess so. Will they have room?"

"I'll ask."

"Are they home now? I could run up with you and see. Then you wouldn't have to call."

She started up the stairs and I limped behind her, supporting myself on the cold, wet, iron railing. Halfway up I turned and looked back at the truck in the parking lot, raising my index finger to Lester to tell her I'd just be a minute. Her arm came out of the driver's window and the hand appeared silhouetted above the cab roof, thumb and forefinger forming a circle. Some of the hollowness inside me filled with gratitude and affection for Lester.

Elkhorn's supercilious cat, Sugar, a vision of feline warmth and luxury, raised her head and looked at us when we came through the door, then retightened her snow-white body into a round coil amid the couch cushions. The apartment was warm and dry, the carpet was thick under foot, and the indirect light from the table lamps at either end of the couch shed a soft, comforting glow over the room. Lisa called Elkhorn, and Kelley's voice answered from the room she and Elkhorn shared. Lisa walked into the hall and toward their room, and I stood in the middle of the carpet, damp and chilled.

Lisa was gone several minutes, and when she came back she gave me a tentative smile. "It's okay with them, but Tina and Jacko are riding with them, too, so it might be kind of crowded...."

"Oh. Well, you're still welcome to go with us. I know Lester'd like to have you."

"She would?"

"Sure. She really likes you. She talks to you easier than to just about anybody else, for one thing."

"Well...."

"Come with us."

"Well, that's what I told Kathy I was going to do...."

"So come on."

"All right." She smiled a little ruefully. "I have a hard time resisting you, Milam."

"It's mutual. It's real mutual."

We stood there five or six feet apart, able neither to embrace nor to turn away. "Well," I finally said, "suppose we pick you up about five-thirty, then?"

"Fine. I'll be ready."

"Fine." I started for the door, and she followed. As I was going out, she said, "And, Cass?"

"Yeah?"

"Get Lester to clean up that ankle, huh?"

"I'll see what kind of a doctor she is." She closed the door behind me, and I limped down the stairs.

Chapter 20

Lester was as gentle as she could be with my wound, but it still hurt a good bit when she cleaned it for me. She soaked it a long time in hot, soapy water and then carefully sponged it off and bandaged it. I endured it like a good butch and tried not to jerk and yell. I mostly succeeded. I'd told her Lisa was still riding with us in the morning and she seemed glad, but she hadn't tried to pry into anything else that might have gone on between Lisa and me. Instead, she treated me carefully, as if she was afraid I might break under normal conversation. I let her.

She fixed us supper, two Night Hawk steak and corn frozen dinners apiece and a salad, and she washed the few dishes involved after settling me in the living room with my ankle propped up in front of the heater and a beer in my hand. I had to keep reminding myself that it was Lester who needed watching out for, that I wasn't the one going to Dallas tomorrow to bury my lover. I thought she must be glad to have something to do, and that by taking care of me she could take her mind off her own sadness.

It was hard for me to keep from thinking about Lisa, though. We'd always had these differences, and we both knew it, but we had so many other positive things going for us that this philosophical difference hadn't seemed to matter too much. Now, though, with Lisa having an affair with Kathy, whose views of lesbianism and feminism stood in stark contrast to mine, it looked like this thing might be enough to break us up. I should have made a deeper commitment to Lisa a long time ago, I thought. Then this wouldn't be happening to us. But I knew that wasn't necessarily true. I couldn't tie Lisa to me, and I didn't want to. If she wanted out, I'd have to let her, no matter what our agreement was. And as it stood, I didn't have any right to complain at all. We were both doing what we'd agreed, in a very lesbian-feminist way, to do. I wanted to talk to somebody, and not just Lester. I got up and hobbled to the phone to call Jacko.

It was so good, I thought as I dialed her number, to have Jacko for a friend. The apartment where she'd lived for twelve years was the one in which she and I had first made love, the day she'd moved in, when I was needing that kind of a friend and was delighted to find that she was, too. I still remembered that night with pleasure and gratitude. So, I thought, did she. I always felt welcome in that place.

The phone rang and Jacko, for once, answered in person instead of letting her machine get it.

"Hey, babe," I said as cheerfully as I could.

"Hey, lady! I was just about to call you. Guess what!"

"What?"

"It's official!"

"What's official?"

"Tina and I are tying the knot."

"What?"

"We're moving in together."

"Hey, great!" I said with forced enthusiasm.

"Isn't it? And we're getting a duplex!"

"You are? She's not moving in there?"

"No. I'm getting out of this hole at last. We signed the lease today. You've got to see it! It's great! Two bedrooms, a dining room, a huge living room, a humongous bath with a tub *and* a separate shower, and—" she paused dramatically—"a fireplace!"

"Wow."

"I can't wait for you to see it."

"I can't either. Maybe when we get back from Dallas."

"You bet! Listen, sweetheart, I've got to run. We were just on our way out the door. But I'll see you tomorrow, okay?"

"Yeah, babe. See you up there."

"You be careful on the road, you hear?"

"I will," I said. "You, too."

I told Lester about Jacko's news, and she looked at me speculatively and said, "You okay?"

"Sure," I told her, trying to sound puzzled. "My ankle hurts some, is all."

"Uh," said Lester. I was afraid I wasn't fooling her. Jacko's moving was another change in my life, when what I wanted was something to depend on. And now she'd always be with Tina, too, even when I needed her alone.

"Well," I said. "We've got to be up early, so let's get to bed, how about?"

"Okay." She went around turning off lights and checking the doors without further comment. We took our turns in the bathroom, Lester going first, and when I came into the bedroom, she had the bed all turned down for us and was standing beside it. "Get in and I'll cover you up," she said. I did, carefully, guarding my bandaged ankle from hitting the edge of the mattress, and Lester lifted the covers and drew them over me as if I'd been made of glass. Then she went to the light switch by the door, said, "Holler if you need anything," and flipped off the light.

"Hey!" I said. "Where are you going?"

"Couch."

"Lester, come on. You aren't going to hurt me. You sleep right here."

"Well . . . you sure?"

"Lester, I don't much want to be alone tonight." I didn't realize until I said it how much I really meant it.

She came back across the room in the dark and eased herself under the covers with me, lying rigid on the far side of the bed. I laughed. "It's like the old lesbian-spending-the-night-with-straight-friend syndrome. Don't

you think you could get over that way another third of an inch without falling off?"
"Fuck." Lester never took kindly to teasing.
"Come on, relax."
"Well, hell. Lisa won't like it."
"Lisa won't—? Is that why you were sleeping on the couch? Listen, babe, our sleeping together has nothing to do with Lisa, okay?"
"Uh-huh. That's not the way I figure."
I thought about it. "Lester," I said, "Lisa's the one that moved you in here in the first place. Now, do you think she'd have done that if she'd minded our sleeping together?"
"Maybe not *sleeping* together."
"Oh, hell. Lester, I wanted you to make love to me, and not as some kind of substitute for Lisa, either, and I sure as hell liked it, as I presume you know. And I'd love to make love to you, too. If you'd like that sometime."
She didn't answer. I waited, and then I said, "Relax, babe," again. Lester didn't speak or move. I could see she was stiff as a board over there, staring at the ceiling. Her profile in the dark looked very young.
I reached for her, taking hold of her arm to pull her toward me, but she resisted and I lay back. "Okay," I said, "I'm not a rapist, but can't you relax some?"
Lester sighed heavily. "Hell, you got my clothes off of me the other night. That's more than anybody else ever did."
I restrained myself from laughing, and looking at her lying there I was suddenly overwhelmed with tenderness for this young woman that could have been me twenty years ago, uncertain but loving, wanting friendship and affection and passion and not knowing enough yet about how all those things worked together to be sure of her ground, but meeting it all with courage and concern for other people. I moved over and lay on my back beside her, shoulder to shoulder, and took her unresisting hand in mine. "If nobody else ever did that, then I'm honored," I said, "and I won't say another word about it." I squeezed

her hand. "So why don't we move over so you won't fall off in the night, and get some sleep." I moved back to my side of the bed, and Lester, after a minute, followed.

"Cass?" she said. "I . . . what was that you said about controlling a jet fighter with an automatic pilot?"

"The other night? You mean, about how the pilot doesn't really give up control?"

"Yeah."

"What about it?" I turned on my side, raising myself on an elbow so I could look down at her lying on her back, watching me anxiously. She didn't say anything, just looked up at me in the near-darkness, and the look said all I needed to know. I bent toward her slowly, never taking my eyes from hers, giving her time to refuse, to turn aside, but she held my gaze with a frightened kind of determination, and suddenly reached up to pull me down against her. It was a gesture of complete surrender. I kissed her, I touched her, I took her pajamas off of her, all the time holding back, going slow for her, though desire was in me like molten lava. And when I paused with my palm covering her breast, feeling her quickened breathing, and said, "Lester, are you sure?" I finally saw her smile, a smile that transformed the anxious child into a willing lover. "Shut up," she said, "and fly the plane."

Chapter 21

The alarm went off at four-thirty. I groped for it and turned it off. I'd have gone back to sleep, except Lester shook me gently by the shoulder. "Time to get up, Cass," she said.

"Ummm. Okay. In a minute."

"No, now. We've got to load my bike, remember?"

It had gotten a good deal warmer during the night, so that waking up naked was pleasant for a change. Lester reached for the lamp by her side of the bed and turned it on, the pink shade casting a soft glow that made me squint, but only for a moment. Then I got my eyes opened and smiled at Lester. She had kicked off the covers except for the sheet, and that lay loosely across her knees. She stretched, arms above her head, and looked over at me half-shyly, but without any of the awkward self-consciousness I was used to seeing. She looked beautiful.

I wanted to touch her, and more, but she sat up and hopped out of bed. "Come on," she said over her shoulder. "I'll put the coffee on."

By the time we were dressed and outside in the damp, warm air struggling with the motorcycle, we were both soaked with sweat. The damn bike must have weighed about half a ton, and you'd think anything with wheels would have been a lot easier than that thing was to roll up a ramp into the back of a truck. But Lester and I were made of sturdy stuff, and we put our backs into it and got the job done. Lester had never hauled anything in a pickup like this, and I showed her how to tighten the ropes and tie the knots so they'd stay tight but release easily. She leaned over my shoulder to watch, and I was conscious of her breasts pressing against my back through our clothes. I wondered if she was, too. I would have bet on it; she and I were a lot alike.

We went back in and changed clothes, into what we would wear to the funeral. Without discussing it, it turned out we'd agreed on standard dyke attire, Lester in dark grey men's slacks and sport coat with a white dress shirt, dark tie and men's shoes, total drag, and me in black slacks, black knit pullover shirt, and black running shoes. If I'd owned more formal clothes, I'd have worn them for Sharla, but I didn't. I decided I looked okay, and Lester looked dignified and suitably sober as she adjusted her collar and tied her tie in an expert four-in-hand knot. I got my gold labyris tie tack out of my jewelry box and told her, "Try this."

She looked at it, frowned, turning it in her fingers to catch the light, muttered, "Thanks," and pinned her tie with it. I saw she wasn't going to be able to take much kindness today. Now that the reality of the funeral was on us, the pain was too close to the surface. I thought she'd never forgive me if I made her cry.

We left the cats indoors with plenty of food and water and clean kitty litter, and we left Ronson well-supplied with food and water in the back yard. I don't like for the cats to be out when I'm not there, in case one of them might get in some kind of trouble and I wouldn't be there to help. I put coffee in a thermos bottle for the trip, checked my cash and credit cards in my billfold, and we hit the road for Lisa's place.

When we got there, Kelley and Elkhorn and Lisa, and Rachel, their other roommate, were all out in the parking lot loading up for the trip, and I noticed a big Coleman cooler in Kelley's truck. Food or beer or both, I presumed. I'd planned to stop and grab something to eat on the way, somewhere. Tina and Jacko drove up in Tina's old Subaru, piled out, and started transferring miscellaneous sacks and garment bags into Kelley's car. It looked like they planned to stay a week. Lisa had been right; there really wouldn't have been room for her to ride with them. I kissed Jacko and congratulated her on her new apartment and new apartment-mate, and I kissed Tina and told her Jacko was a good catch, which was true, I believed, and it was for sure that nobody else had ever been able to get as far toward catching her as Tina had. All this time Lisa had been busy helping the others load up. Now she came over and said, "Hi," without touching me.

"You ready?" I said, being as neutral as I could.

"Ready," she said.

I stood facing her, feeling awkward. "Well," I said after a pause, "let's get after it."

I went around the driver's side of the truck, leaving Lester and Lisa to work out who was going to sit by the door and who by me. When I got in, Lester had slid over and taken the middle of the seat and Lisa was sitting by the door. Lester was saying, "You can sit here if you want to," and Lisa was protesting that, no, that was all right, and they might trade later on. I suddenly wanted to feel Lisa's body beside mine so badly that I almost groaned aloud. Instead, I gritted my teeth, took a deep breath, let it out, and started the truck without commenting on the seating arrangements. In a slowly thickening ground fog, I pulled out for Dallas.

Chapter 22

"How's your ankle?" Lisa leaned forward to talk around Lester, who was sitting stiffly in the middle of the seat, staring ahead with a forbiddingly stern look.

"I'm going to have it amputated when I get to Dallas."

"That bad, huh?"

"Yeah. You noticed Lester had to carry me this morning. That's why I have her over here; I need her to put on the brake for me if I need to stop. Of course, I don't plan to stop until I get there, so, Lester, you can go to sleep if you want to."

Lester gave me a wan smile.

"It'll save on shoes if you have it amputated, anyway," Lisa said.

"Oh, no. I'm gonna have them put the foot back on the bottom of the leg bone. I guess, while I'm at it, I'll have both sides done, so I'll come out even."

"God, you're awful!" Lisa sounded relieved. "Seriously, though, is it bad?"

"No, not this morning. A little sore, but Lester took good care of me last night. Just what the doctor would have ordered, if I'd been to a doctor."

"Good for you, Lester."

"Uh," Lester said. And then she surprised me by saying, "We take care of each other."

Lisa, no doubt catching all kinds of implications in that, was momentarily silent, and I took my hand off the wheel and slapped Lester affectionately on the leg. "You bet we do," I said.

"Ah, but, you know, Cass," Lisa put in, leading the talk away from dangerous waters, "you really ought to go get a tetanus shot, shouldn't you?"

"Nope. I keep my tetanus shots current, babe. I'm forever getting cuts and puncture wounds out in the wilds of Austin. Hazards of the job."

"Oh. Well, good. I don't have to nag you, then."

A little, wavering flame of hope sprang up in me. If Lisa had planned to nag me about something, maybe it meant she planned to be around enough to nag. God, I hoped she did.

Dawn was on its way, a rosiness of growing brightness making the ground fog, now lying thick in the hollows and over the fields, look like pink cotton candy. Overhead the sky was lightening toward blue with a scattering of fluffy clouds. It was already about seventy degrees. It looked like the cool, rainy spell was over.

Lester in the morning light looked a little drawn and tired. We hadn't gotten just a whole lot of sleep, but it would have been plenty any other time. This funeral, though, wasn't going to be any picnic, especially with Sharla's family so hostile. I devoutly hoped there wouldn't be any trouble.

Lisa, I noticed, didn't look so rested, either. I wondered if she'd lost sleep over me, or if maybe she'd managed to get together with Kathy after I'd left her last night. I remembered some long, sleepless nights Lisa and I'd spent together when we were first getting acquainted, and I wondered if she and Kathy were doing the same things. Or whatever two lesbian-feminists do together, I thought nastily. But then, they probably couldn't imagine what Lester and I could do together. Hell. I guess we all do about the same.

We passed those odd, flat-topped, low hills by the road that I'd heard were the remains of coastal shell reefs from the shallow seas that used to cover this part of Texas. We passed Temple and we passed Waco. By Temple,

Lester had gone to sleep, leaning stiffly sideways with her head on my shoulder. After that, Lisa and I hadn't said much for fear of waking her, and just before Waco Lisa had taken off her jacket, wadded it into a pillow, and settled down in the corner with her eyes closed. Lester shifted stiff muscles, sat up, and asked, "Where are we?" I told her, and she grunted and looked over at Lisa, who opened her eyes and gave her a smile. Then Lisa shifted toward Lester, caught her arm, and pulled her toward her, and they resettled leaning against each other. I drove, trying not to think, and got into Dallas by nine-thirty.

In the oak-shaded parking lot of the funeral home Lester and I unloaded her motorcycle, which came down the ramp a whole lot easier than it had gone up, fortunately for our good clothes.

"Are you going to ride it to the cemetery?" Lisa asked her, and Lester nodded, pressing her lips together. The closer we got to the actual funeral, the harder I could see it was for Lester to hold herself together. We parked the bike on its side stand beside my truck.

Other carloads of dykes from Austin started arriving, and most of us were able to park close together at one side of the parking lot. I looked at the crowd assembling and felt proud of us. We were all types of lesbians, with everything from Lester's drag attire and man's haircut to Tina's black linen dress and high heels. There were dykes in jeans and dykes in pantsuits and dykes with short hair and with long hair and with makeup and without it— we were a good cross-section. We'd be an education to the other people here, if they cared to study us. And there was a good turnout of us, too. Altogether, I counted twenty-three. Amazing, especially for a workday. Kelley and Elkhorn had really done a good job of organizing this.

When everybody that anybody was expecting had showed up, it was nearly time for the funeral to start and there were a good many cars in the lot besides ours. Several of the other mourners had given us strange looks as they'd arrived, but the family entrance was around the back of the place and we hadn't had any direct run-ins, and I was relieved about that. I'd been harboring the fear that we'd get up here and have some of Sharla's relatives cause a scene, and while we were glad to be seen as dykes mourning our friend, we weren't here for a demonstration, except a demonstration of our love for one of our own. Elkhorn, looking alien in a grey-green pantsuit and matching pumps and with lipstick on, took the lead and suggested it was time to go in, and we trooped off to the front door of the place in a quiet mob.

We went through the door, sinking at once into deep carpet, and walked into the big, flower-smelling, semi-dark room with pews in it like a church, and nobody tried to stop us or say a thing. A few heads turned when we came in; one or two people leaned toward their neighbors and whispered. That was all. The atmosphere was heavy and solemn. We found two pews toward the back of the room and filed in, me following Lisa with Lester behind me, and sat down. It was very still, even with all those people. There weren't even the faint rustlings you hear when you're waiting for church to start, no audible whispers or giggles, no shuffling of paper, no scuffling of feet. There were a lot of flowers down at the front, and the coffin was already there, closed, I was relieved to see, with a blanket of white carnations on it. I felt Lester move beside me and her warm thigh, which had been pressing against mine in the too-cool auditorium's air-conditioning, pulled away and left a cold spot on my leg. I turned my head slightly, to look at her without being so direct about it that I'd intrude on her grief, and she was gone.

I jerked around, then, and just caught a vanishing glimpse of her back, disappearing out the door. I stood up quickly, startling Lisa, who looked up alarmed, but I didn't have time to explain. I hurried up the aisle and out the door just as the somber-suited usher was closing it. Behind me, I heard the organ music start.

"Lester!" I spotted her striding across the parking lot toward her bike. She didn't turn, if she heard me. I ran after her, glad for the millionth time that I don't wear women's shoes, and caught her as she was swinging her leg over the seat of the motorcycle.

She looked up at me with a set expression, and I could see she was having a hell of a time controlling herself. I didn't know what to say, so I didn't say anything. She looked away from me, the muscles in her jaws working, and then she turned on the ignition key of her bike and hit the starter button. The engine came to life and began idling roughly, too cold to drive right away.

"Where are you going?" I said.

"Nowhere." She cracked the throttle a little to warm the engine faster.

"Can I go with you?"

She shook her head.

"Are you coming back here?"

"Okay."

"I don't know how long this'll take."

She looked at her watch. "I'll meet you back here at noon," she said. Her voice was hoarse with grief. She started walking the motorcycle backwards out of the parking place, turning it toward the street. I walked along, and just before she left, I reached out and touched her arm. "I'm okay, just let me go," she said quickly through clenched teeth, and I stepped back as she put the bike in gear and pulled away. I watched her stop at the street, check the traffic, and ride off, turning at the next corner and going out of sight behind a building that blocked my view. I went back to the funeral home and slipped back into a back pew by myself. I was wishing I hadn't watched Lester out of sight. I don't really, rationally think there's anything to that belief, but hers was a ship I definitely wanted to see returning to me.

The preacher, I supposed he was the one from Sharla's parents' church, was a blond guy about fifty years old wearing a business suit. He kept flashing an inappropriate smile as he read, jerkily, through passage after passage of Bible verses. I couldn't make much sense of the ones he'd selected, either; none of them seemed to fit together or fit the situation very well. Everybody sat and listened to them as if they did.

Lisa, a couple of rows in front of me, kept turning her head to look back, but I was too directly behind her for her to see me. I finally slid down to the end of my pew, and she saw me right away. I nodded to tell her things were okay, and she smiled discreetly in answer. I thought about going down and sitting beside her, but I didn't.

Another preacher — maybe this one was the one from Sharla's parents' church and the other one was somebody else — got up and started talking about Sharla. Only he wasn't talking about Sharla, really. He was talking about a beloved daughter and a devout churchgoer who'd served as a leader of her youth group and who'd been a good student with a bright future ahead of her. He talked about all her relatives and friends at home missing her, but how they ought to take heart because God moved in mysterious ways, and this thing wasn't "given into our understanding." No shit, I thought. And nobody but Lester was even very curious about how it all happened. Even she seemed to be at a dead end. But somebody met Sharla that night, and after that meeting, Sharla was either in a hurry or upset or maybe just real unlucky, and she went off the road through that guardrail and died. Some act of God.

I thought about the Sharla I knew. Lesbian-feminist who really tried to stick to her principles, but still an elitist who thought Lisa was way too good for me. And yet somebody who could love Lester enough to be her lover, to live with her, to go out with her in the company of friends who might not approve of Lester's youth and drag-butch ways. I remembered Lester's saying, "She hated loving me." But she did love her, all the same. Because, I told myself, who could help loving Lester? I certainly did.

The preacher wound up his sermon without once mentioning that Sharla was a lesbian, of course. He didn't speak of the women in Austin who'd been her friends, who'd danced with her and drunk beer with her, who'd argued feminist politics with her long into the night, who'd made love with her, supported her when she needed support and been supported by her when things were rough with them. Twenty-two of us were sitting right there in front of him, but we were invisible to these hets who thought they'd owned Sharla and who thought they now owned all the right to grieve for her. I got angrier and angrier. And poor Lester, too broken up by Sharla's loss even to stay here, out somewhere now in a strange town alone, and all she'd gotten from Sharla's family was gross insult and the threat of arrest. I felt like standing up and yelling, forcing these ignorant stuffed-shirts to acknowledge us in some way, if only to try to kick us out. Of course, I didn't.

It was over, finally, and six men took hold of the fancy bronze coffin and rolled it on its wheeled dolly up the aisle and out the door where the hearse had been backed up to receive it. After that, the ushers indicated the rest of us could leave, and we did, the lesbians leading the way. I caught Lisa's hand and swung in beside her as she came by, and she squeezed my fingers hard. She'd been crying. I tucked her arm through mine.

We gathered by our cars, a quiet group, some with tear tracks on their faces, others smiling nervously, or hiding emotion by trying to look unconcerned.

"Where's Lester?" Kelley asked me.

"She couldn't take it. She's okay. She's meeting me back here at noon."

"Let's go, babe," Lisa said, and I opened the door for her and she got into the truck.

We filed out of the parking lot, the lesbian contingent once again leading, right behind the cars with Sharla's immediate family. Kelley had scooted into the line right there, in front of some other relative of Sharla's in a Cadillac who hadn't been quick enough on the trigger to block her, and the rest of us crowded in right on her bumper. A funeral home employee at the driveway told each of us as we passed to turn our headlights on. We drove slowly through the streets of Dallas with motorcycle cops holding traffic for us at the intersections, and the cemetery turned out to be pretty close. We parked along the little roads that divided off sections of graves.

This wasn't much like the last cemetery I'd been in, a little graveyard down on the coast where somebody I loved was buried, but it brought back memories just the same. Lisa knew it and put her arm around me as we walked toward the green canvas awning set up beside the grave they'd dug for Sharla. They had hurried with the flowers from the funeral home and had them lying all around the hole, and they'd covered up the piles of fresh dirt with blankets of Astroturf, but it was still a grave, and they were going to put Sharla's body in there and cover it up with dirt, and I could see I wasn't going to like this part at all.

They were seating the family in folding chairs, but there were so many relatives there that a lot of them were going to have to stand, too. There were a couple of old people, a man and a woman that had to be helped carefully across the grass and seated. They looked more distressed than anybody else there. I wondered who they were. Lisa and I stood just behind the last row of chairs, and her arm around my waist was good to feel.

Then the second preacher, the one who'd given the sermon, said a prayer or two, and that was that. People started drifting off. I looked around for Lester, but she hadn't shown. It was only eleven now; I wondered if she'd come here after everybody else was gone, or if it was just all too much for her and she was maybe off drinking beer or something. I was worried about her.

A bunch of the Austin dykes wanted to get something to eat, and I felt like I ought to be hungry, since I hadn't stopped, after all, for breakfast, so I went along. Lisa and I talked, on the way to a cafeteria Tina was leading us to, about the funeral. She'd felt a lot of the same things I had, naturally. We both felt frustrated and unsatisfied. The funeral hadn't served the purpose for us of a formal parting with Sharla, the way I assume it had for

Sharla's family. Instead, we were left angry and restless and sad. Conversation at lunch showed everybody felt the same way.

"Look," Kelley said. "This is no good. Why don't we all get together at the bar tonight and drink some beer and have our own memorial party?"

Agreement was enthusiastic and unanimous. On that note we separated, wishing each other a good trip and telling all our drivers to be careful. Lisa and I got in the truck and headed back to the funeral home. It was time to meet Lester, and I was getting real nervous about not knowing where she was.

The asphalt parking lot around the funeral home was wide and empty. I parked where I had before, at the side under an oak tree, and we waited. After a few minutes, I told Lisa I was going to sit in the back so I could watch better. So I let down the tailgate and we both sat there, and in a couple of minutes Lester rode up. I heaved a sigh of relief. I wanted to hug her, but I could see by her face I'd better not. Lisa did it, though, and Lester wrapped her arms around Lisa and held on for dear life. Then she got off her bike, she and I loaded it and tied it down tight, and we pulled out for Austin. Lester sat in the middle again. I think she wanted to be surrounded by friends. Lisa kept an arm around her or a hand on her leg or touched her in some way all the way back, but we kept the conversation light and even managed a few laughs, so that by the time we'd gotten home, we all felt close and easy with each other, and when we let Lisa off at her place, I got out of the truck and kissed her goodbye. It almost seemed like everything was going to be all right. Kathy hadn't even showed up at the funeral.

Chapter 23

We changed out of our funeral clothes together, and when we were both down to our underwear I went to Lester and kissed her, enjoying the feel of her muscular body in my arms and the familiar softness of her lips on mine. It wasn't a passionate kiss, just a loving one.

"Were you okay alone in Dallas?" I asked her.

"Yeah." She averted her eyes and turned away, pulling a tee shirt out of the dresser drawer.

"Good." I waited to see if she'd volunteer anything about what she'd done, but I knew Lester by now, and it didn't surprise me that she kept her mouth shut. "I worried about you a little, but I knew you could take care of yourself."

"Yeah, I can take care of myself." She pulled the shirt over her head and stepped into a pair of jeans. "Lisa's sure nice," she said.

"Yeah."

"I can't stand that Kathy."

"Oh, well. Lisa likes her, so she must be okay."

"I guess so." She buckled her belt, then looked up with a fierce expression. "But if she's so goddamn nice, how come she's trying to take Lisa away from you? I think she's a shithead."

I grinned at her. "I don't own Lisa, you know. And anyway, I'm not a bit sure she's trying to take Lisa away from me. She's just sleeping with her, just like I am with you. Lisa and I've always agreed we could do this if we wanted to."

"Yeah, but—hell." She sat on the bed and put on her heavy socks and motorcycle boots. "You want to go with me somewhere?"

"Where?"

"Out to 2222."

"Why?"

"I'm meeting Rowderburr."

"What?"

Lester sighed a long-suffering sigh. "Cass you *heard* me. I said I'm meeting Rowderburr, and I want you to go with me. I called from Dallas to set it up."

"You're meeting Ellen out there?"

"No."

"Well, then, I don't understand. You're going out there and then meeting her somewhere else?"

"Just get your pants on, and put on some boots. You better wear a jacket, too. You can use Sharla's helmet."

I did as I was told and quit asking questions. We unloaded the motorcycle and I strapped on Sharla's helmet, which fit me, amazingly enough. I'd been sure it would be too big, since my head's smaller than most. "Lester," I said as I climbed on the seat behind her, "will you tell me where you're meeting Ellen, so in case I fall off the back of this thing I can just walk and meet you there?"

"I'm not."

"What? I mean, you're not? Well, then, what the—"

"I'm meeting *Rod* Rowderburr. The fag. Ape-arms."

"But—"

"Got your feet on the pegs? Okay, keep 'em there. Hang on to me, and don't try to lean when we turn, or you'll kill us. Hang on."

We pulled smoothly out of the driveway and headed up Hank Street, me with a death-grip on Lester and a grin on my face. I didn't know where we were going or why, but I already knew I was going to love getting there.

Lester got on Ben White, and I got a new perspective on Austin traffic. On a motorcycle you're right out there in it, and if any of those cars even bump you, it's your own, flesh-and-blood body that will be taking the blow.

I hadn't felt so exposed since that time I dreamed I went to Rylander's naked to buy a box of Tampax. It was downright scary. But it was also very exciting, and I got a kick out of being one of two butch dykes on a motorcycle out there in front of god and everybody, looking tough and stereotypical and cheering up any lesbians who might be driving by. I got to wondering if I could get Lester to teach me how to drive this thing alone. How hard could it be? I can drive a truck and a tractor.

Lester took Ben White out past Lamar and got on MoPac, headed north. It was a wonderful ride with not much traffic going our way, but my hands were freezing from the wind chill, and I slipped them under Lester's jacket. That helped. Lester took the R.R. 2222 exit and we began riding the swooping curves that make that road so beautiful and so dangerous. I noticed right away that the bike could take these curves better than a car could, feeling in harmony with the road rather than fighting it. I wondered why we'd come this way, rather than stay on Loop 360, which was what Ben White became after it crossed Lamar, but now I saw that Lester was taking us past the place where Sharla had gone off into the lake. She slowed for that curve, with its beautiful view of the Bull Creek arm of Lake Austin, and I noticed a new metal section of guardrail, shinier than the rest of it, that told its own story. I tightened my grip around Lester's waist, and then we were through the curve and crossing 360, still heading west.

We were getting out of town pretty well, away from the housing developments and convenience stores, when Lester slowed down and turned into an unpaved road that ran steeply down through the cedar brake into a valley. It twisted and turned, and then suddenly it ended at a stone house with a red Corvette parked in front of it. Lester stopped, and we got off.

"Rowderburr's retreat," Lester said. "Come on." She strode toward the front door.

"Wait a minute!" I caught up with her and caught

her by the arm. "What are we here for? Shouldn't you fill me in?"

"Sharla met this guy that night. I figured it out. We're gonna find out what happened."

"What?" I said, but Lester was out of my grip and already knocking on the door.

The tall guy with the black hair opened the door. He didn't look too good. A slant of late-afternoon sunlight caught him full in the face and he blinked, peering at us against the glare. He looked wary and a little bedraggled, not the sharp-dressing leather freak or the casual cowboy, but just a guy with trouble on his mind. "You must be Celeste," he said.

Lester grunted, and I said, "I'm Cass," and he stepped back and let us inside.

The place was mostly one big room, kind of a hunting lodge effect, with limestone walls and a big fireplace with a cedar mantel set in the rockwork. It was masculine and comfortable, and I'd have given a pretty penny to stay here with a lover for a weekend, if I'd had a pretty penny. Rowderburr waved us to seats on a leather couch, and he stood beside the hearth, facing us like a prisoner facing a jury. It was a lot like the scene with his wife at the Silverman Ranch, only she looked relatively innocent and he looked guilty as sin.

"I'm sorry," Rowderburr said. He shook his head. "I've felt bad about it ever since it happened, but I didn't see what good it would do if I told everybody about it. It wouldn't bring her back."

"Why'd she come out here?" Lester demanded.

"I asked her to."

"Well, go on!" Lester was impatient.

"Okay. Look, Celeste, I didn't mean anybody any harm, okay? But when she saw me in that bar in Houston, dressed like that, she knew right away that I belonged there. There was no way I could pass for a tourist, see?"

"So what? Who cares if you're queer?"

"My wife doesn't know it, and that's who cares." He picked up a glass from the mantel, looked at the trace of liquid in the bottom, and put it back down. "Look, would y'all like a drink?"

"No. Just go on with the story. We haven't got all night."

"Well," he said, looking regretfully at the glass again, "I just didn't want her to find out, that's all."

"Goddammit, will you go on and tell it? What the fuck do you care if the world knows you're a fag? You're getting a divorce, anyway, aren't you?"

"Okay. Look. It's the ranch, see? The ranch belongs to Ellen's father."

"So?"

"So I'm his fair-haired boy, right? I married Ellen after he made me foreman of the ranch. Silverman loves me like a son, see?"

"Yeah?"

"Yeah, he does. So now Ellen and I are splitting, and he thinks Ellen's a bitch to get rid of me. So he's keeping me on, see, and Ellen's going to have to move off the place. Because he doesn't want her around instead of me. He wants me to stay. Get it?"

"Yeah," said Lester, "I get it. So if Ellen finds out you're queer, she tells her old man and he kicks you out instead of her."

"Right. So all I wanted was for Sharla to say she wouldn't tell Ellen about me. I mean, god, she was a lesbian, so I thought she'd keep my secret, you know? But she said she couldn't promise. Hell, I wish to god I'd never met her before, but Ellen introduced us one time before we started splitting up. That's how she knew me at the bar. God, I wish I'd never gone there. But how the hell was I to know one of my wife's classmates was going to show up in Houston at a men's bar? But anyway, I called her in Austin the next day to ask her not to give me away, and damned if she didn't start telling me all this stuff about sisterhood and how she and I might both be gay, but she and Ellen were both women, and all that kind of stuff. So she finally said she'd think about it. So I called her the next day, and she still didn't know. So then the next day I called her again and she said she was meeting Ellen at the library and she thought she'd tell her, because women had to stick together. Do you know what that would have meant to me? Not only do I lose my job if this comes out, but I even lose this place — it belongs to the old man, too — and who knows how it'll affect the divorce settlement? So, anyway, she agreed to come out here and talk it out in person before she told Ellen. And that's why she came out here, and when she left, that's when the accident happened. So now I guess you-all are going to tell Ellen, aren't you?"

Lester was staring at Rowderburr as if she could look a hole through him. "Sharla was still gonna tell?"

"Yeah, she was. Sisterhood, she said."

"Rowderburr, tell the truth. You might as well, because people know what we know and where we are, and you can't kill us and cover it up. You killed Sharla, didn't you?"

I stared at Lester. In the first place, I couldn't see how an accident like Sharla's could have been faked well enough not to arouse the suspicions of the police, and in the second place, I was horrified to think that, if Lester had a good reason to think that had been done, she'd let us come out here in the middle of nowhere without telling anybody about it, and I was pretty certain she hadn't told. I'd been with her just about night and day except for that couple of hours in Dallas.

"Lester," I said, "for god's sake—"

"Tell me," Lester said, ignoring me.

Rowderburr shook his head. "Celeste, I'm telling you the truth. It was an accident. I saw it happen. Look. She left here in a hurry, that's true. But the reason was that she was trying to make it back to campus in time to catch Ellen and talk to her. So I decided I was going to be there for that meeting, and I jumped in my car and lit out right behind her. And I mean to tell you, that woman was driving like a bat out of hell. Well, my car'll do that on this road, but that VW of hers wasn't made for it, and I was afraid she was going to lose it before she did, a couple of times. So I honked my horn, trying to get her to stop, because I really was scared she was going to get hurt, but she didn't stop, and then we hit that curve there at Bull Creek, and she lost it and went right over. By the time I got to her, she was dead."

"You were the one who climbed down the cliff?" I said.

He nodded.

"You tried to save her?" Lester said.

"Of course I did." He looked miserable. "Of course I did. God, it was my fault, wasn't it? Really. Of course I tried. But I couldn't. I couldn't. She was dead."

Lester said nothing. Rowderburr stood there staring at his boots, the same way he had when I'd surprised him and Sharla in the Orchid Room. The silence lengthened. The fire danced in little yellow flames along the tops of the oak logs in the fireplace, and a red coal dropped into the bed of embers.

Now the decision was ours. We had all the information that Sharla had had, plus the damning facts about how Sharla had died. Sharla had decided in favor of Ellen. But it hadn't been just sisterhood. Sharla had been working toward a love affair with Ellen. The real question, it seemed to me, was whether or not to put ammunition against a gay man in the hands of a queer-hater. To me there was no question. I could never do that. I thought Lester couldn't either. She stood up and looked up at Rod Rowderburr.

"I loved Sharla," she said.

He nodded.

"I don't think you killed her. Nobody did."

He let his eyes meet hers.

"I don't like you. I don't like men much, anyway."

"Ellen's at the ranch, if you want to call her."

Lester shook her head.

"You're going to tell her, though."

"No," Lester said. She walked to the door, and I got up and followed her. We left Rowderburr standing there.

Chapter 24

We stayed at the memorial party at the bar until closing time. Lester and I both drank way too much beer. I hardly remember all the details of the evening. I do remember crying in Lisa's arms at one point, and I remember dancing with Lester with such abandon that people yelled and whistled, and I remember thinking that when Lester and I got home we'd make love all the rest of the night. As it worked out, though, Lester was too drunk even to consider driving her motorcycle home, and she just turned around and handed me her keys. I couldn't drive it either, of course, since even if I'd been sober, I wouldn't have known how. So Kelley loaded me and Lester and Lisa and Kathy all in her car and took us to my house, where Lisa got my truck and drove it back to the bar to get the motorcycle, Kathy riding in the front with her, me and Lester riding together in the back, singing. Several dykes in the bar parking lot loaded the bike for us, since we were beyond doing it, and Lisa and Kathy drove us home and rode off with Kelley or somebody. At least, they weren't still there in the morning.

The rest of the week passed quickly, except for the horrible hangover I had on Tuesday, when Cheryll had to do all the driving and most of the work on putting in winter bedding plants. Lester was out job-hunting every day and had a couple of prospects, but she wouldn't talk about them. I figured she was afraid she'd queer her luck if she did.

The stretch between Monday night and Friday evening did have some highlights. The first one was Tuesday morning. Lester and I were trying to get out of bed, after a night of sleeping like the dead instead of making passionate love. I felt like something the cat had drug in. I was sitting on the edge of the bed with my head in my hands, and I noticed a white gauze bandage on Lester's ankle.
"What's that?" I asked her, pointing to it.
"Nothing."
"What is it, Lester?"
She bent down and peeled it off, revealing a fresh tattoo. It was the initials S.L.D. with a little labyris above them.
"I'll be damned," I said. "Sharla's initials?"
"Uh-huh."
"You got that in Dallas?"
"Yeah."
I didn't know what to say. Sharla had a living memorial, now. For a minute, I thought I'd cry. I finally said, "Did it hurt?"
"Not much."
"How long did it take?"
"Just a few minutes."
"I'll be damned. What did you tell the guy about the labyris? Did he ask about it?"
"Yeah. I showed him your tie tack. I told him it was the sacred ax of the Goddess."
"I'll bet that threw him."
"I don't think you can throw those guys."
"Well. I like it."
"She shouldn't have died."
"No, she shouldn't."
"I'm gonna make coffee."
Then, on Wednesday, Kelley and Elkhorn came by the house just as I was getting in from work. I gave them a beer and we sat in the back yard.
"I talked to Lisa last night," Kelley said. "She's worried about you, Cass."

"I'm okay."

"She just needs you to give her some space, you know? She doesn't know what to think about anything right now."

"Did she send you to tell me this?"

"No. Did you know she's looking for a job?"

"No. What kind of a job?" But I knew the answer.

"Something in human services. She wants to use her degree, finally."

"I hope she can."

"She was furious with Kathy for letting the dog bite you."

"Oh, yeah? That's not what she told me."

"Yeah, she was. Kathy said it was because Alice thought you were a man. Lisa told her nobody could be more of a woman than you are."

"I guess that's a compliment."

"You know it is. She loves you, Cass."

"I know that. I just don't know what that means."

And on Thursday, Lester got a job at the plastics plant where Lisa worked. She gave Lisa as a reference, and they hired her on the spot. They told her to start work Monday morning. She invited Lisa over for supper and fixed us chicken-fried steaks, and we all had a good time, and then Lisa went home early, and I didn't quite dare to ask why. Lester and I cleaned up the kitchen together and went to bed early, ourselves.

And Friday night was the annual Halloween dance. This is the big one of the year, the all-woman costume dance at the Unitarian Church. I didn't go in costume, and neither did Lester, just her standard drag. If I'd had a suit, I would have gone in drag, too. We'd have made a cute couple. Anyway, I danced with more women than there were dances, because a lot of the time we danced in threes and fours. The woman who won the costume contest was dressed as a flasher, in an overcoat with absolutely nothing underneath, as she demonstrated over and over in millisecond flashes, to the howls and whistles of the audience. Lisa and I were a little careful around each other, and I made a special effort to speak to Kathy and be as nice as I could, and she made the same effort for me. She wasn't so bad, really. But I wanted Lisa back, bad. At least she hadn't moved in with Kathy yet. I didn't know what I'd do if she did.

I drank very cautiously, about three beers all night, and I was ready to leave by about eleven. It had been a long week. Lester, I noticed, was dancing a lot with a nice-looking, very young woman I didn't know. When I told her I was going home, she said, "I think I'll stay awhile."

"Have a good time," I told her.

She gave me a dazzling smile.

It was turning cooler again. November was in the air. I was just as glad to see this October end. I drove home alone, parked in the driveway, and went up to the front door. Some perceptive young neighbor of mine had propped the screen open with a rock and written "Bulldike" across the door at an angle from top to bottom in orange spray paint. It showed up nicely in the light of the porch light. You could read it quite well from the street.

I went back to the garage where I had some cans of paint. I found some white that would match the door, then put it down and picked up some orange that I'd used last summer to paint a lawn mower. I took it around the front and shook it until the ball in it had rattled for a full minute. I was going to take care of this right now. No use waiting. I took aim with the spray can and neatly changed the "i" in "Bulldike" to "y."

"Happy Halloween," I said.

I went inside and went to bed to read myself to sleep. I'd been saving up a good paperback mystery.

I shut my mind to the thought of Lisa and Kathy and what they'd be doing tonight after the dance. I did wonder briefly if Lester would go home with her new friend that she'd been dancing with so much, or maybe bring her here and make out on the couch, being careful not to wake Mama Milam. I grinned to myself at the thought. I remember what it was like to be a teenager in love.

I was just shutting my book and reaching for the switch of the bedside lamp, when I heard a car door in the driveway. Lester's friend must have a car, I thought. Then, instead of the sound of Lester's key in the lock, there was a knock on the door. I crawled out and went to see about it.

It was Lisa.

"Did somebody do this while you were at the dance?" she said, gesturing toward the spray-painted door.

"Yeah. Gift from an admirer. Just a little tribute from the neighborhood. Is that all you wanted, or are you going to come in?"

She looked me in the eye, a long, level gaze. "Do you want me to?"

"Yeah. Hell, yes."

I stepped back and let her in. We stood without speaking for a minute, there in the open door, with the warmth of the house on one side of us and the chill of the last October night of the year on the other.

"I thought you'd be with Kathy," I said.

She shook her head. "I thought you'd ask me to leave with you."

"I didn't think you wanted me to."

Lisa smiled and shook her head again. "Milam," she said, "once in a while you give up too easy."

"Well, hell," I said. When we kissed, it was like coming home.

In the morning, when I started out to get the paper, I found Lester curled up on the couch, wrapped in a blanket she must have slipped in and gotten out of the bedroom closet after Lisa and I were asleep. I thought she must have had a good time at the dance; she was sleeping with a smile on her face. I stood looking down at her, feeling peaceful and happy. Then I tiptoed past her and opened the door to look out on the first, sweet morning of November.

OTHER BOOKS FROM BANNED BOOKS

Dreams of the Woman Who Loved Sex,
   Tee Corinne $7.95
Death Strip,
   Benita Kirkland $8.95
A Cry in the Desert,
   Jed A. Bryan $9.95

BANNED BOOKS
Number 231, P.O. Box 33280, Austin, Texas 78764